Sven Diamond was everything his name suggested—hard, cold and with a sharp cutting edge. He knew what he wanted and he usually got it. But was that any reason why Tay should let him order her around?

Another book you will enjoy
by ANGELA CARSON

THE FACE OF THE STRANGER

Fashion photographer Rane had taken against
Greville York from the very first moment she
had met him at Leo d'Arvel's Spring
Collection—so she was dismayed to find that
her next assignment would be at Greville's
house! And if Greville thought he was going to
prevent his young ward Marion marrying Lee,
then Rane was going to do all she could to
thwart him!

GATHERING
OF EAGLES

BY

ANGELA CARSON

MILLS & BOON LIMITED
15–16 BROOK'S MEWS
LONDON W1A 1DR

*First published in Great Britain 1986
by Mills & Boon Limited*

© Angela Carson 1986

*Australian copyright 1986
Philippine copyright 1987
This edition 1987*

ISBN 0 263 75575 4

*Set in Times 10 on 10¼ pt.
01-0287-55385*

*Computer typeset by SB Datagraphics,
Colchester, Essex*

*Printed and bound in Great Britain by
Collins, Glasgow*

CHAPTER ONE

'WE'RE broke, Tay. Hilliard Engineering is finished, unless we can get financial backing to launch our new car.'

Morgan Hilliard's voice held the flat finality of near defeat, something so alien to the sturdy little Northerner that his tone shocked Tay almost as much as his words.

'Do you mean we're *bankrupt*?' she cried.

She had to force the words out through stiff lips, that in the darkness of the luxurious touring car had gone suddenly white.

'Not quite. Not yet,' her father replied, still in the same awful, flat voice, and Tay thought wildly, it can't be true. I must be dreaming.

But the car was real enough. Her father's familiar figure in the driving seat was real. It was only his voice, and the unbelievable things it was saying, that had this nightmarish quality of unreality as it continued remorselessly,

'I saw Northcroft a few days ago.' Northcroft was the firm's accountant and legal adviser, a man whose judgement on commercial affairs was unquestioned. 'He said the bank weren't able to extend our credit, because of the recession. It's hitting everybody, not just us. But it means that we can't finance the tooling for the new car body.'

'But we've already got the new engine in production,' Tay protested. 'You said yourself, it's light-years ahead of anything else on the market now.'

'No matter how advanced it is, an engine isn't of much use if we can't afford to build the body-shells to house it,'

Morgan Hilliard pointed out, and Tay said faintly,

'I never suspected. Why didn't you tell me?'

Tay was actively involved in the working of their family firm, but Morgan Hilliard held the reins, and dealt with the financial side, and nothing had led her to suspect that anything was amiss.

If her father had seemed abstracted just lately, it was nothing unusual. Tay had merely put it down to the fact that his brilliant engineer's mind was formulating some new design or improvement to their already superb product, and she had seen no reason to question him about it.

'I hoped something might come of my contacts at the Federation Dinner tonight,' Morgan Hilliard confessed, and added, with a wry twist of his lips that was a travesty of his usual warm smile. 'I didn't want to spoil the evening for you. You'd been looking forward to it. And it might be the last Federation Dinner we'll attend.'

The Federation Dinner.

The glittering, annual occasion at which the heads of all the major vehicle manufacturers gathered for a social evening, and to which Tay had accompanied her father unquestioningly tonight.

It seemed like another world, now. Looking back, she realised the pointers had been there that evening, but in her ignorance she had not recognised them.

'Your father and Scott Fielding seem deep in conversation,' her dinner partner had observed. 'Scott doesn't usually lavish his attentions on anyone, unless he wants something from them. I wonder what he's after?'

'Why should he be after anything?' Tay had parried. 'He might just be exchanging pleasantries with Dad. Surely that's what this gathering is all about? To give people the opportunity to meet and mix socially, away from the cut-and-thrust of business?'

'If you believe that, you'll believe anything,' Michael

Burk had said. 'The intrigues that go on at this jamboree would put MI5 in the shade.'

'I'm sure my father isn't intriguing with anyone,' Tay had laughed, and said, to divert her companion's attention away from her parent and the man he was talking to, 'I've only ever met Mr Fielding and his wife. I've never seen the other members of their Board.'

'You weren't likely to,' Burk had replied. 'I've never known them to turn up in force like this before.'

'How many of them are there?'

'Three more, besides Scott.' The meal had finished, and broken up, but Michael Burk had remained attached to Tay's side as they strolled through into the next room for coffee and drinks.

'That's the Fielding Financial Director, standing by himself in the far corner.' He had directed Tay's eyes to a lean, unsmiling figure, with coal-black hair slicked down over an unusually long, narrow head, and with his eyes covered by large tinted spectacles, 'Andrew Gleeson,' he had identified the man.

'Anything less like glee would be hard to imagine,' Tay had grimaced. The man reminded her shudderingly of a snake. 'Is that his wife with him?'

'Gleeson's married to his figures.' Burke had shaken his head. 'He's a walking calculating machine, and just about as human. I'd give a lot to know what goes on behind those dark glasses of his. No, the bottle blonde standing next to him is Lance Poulton's wife, Olive. Lance is the man with fair hair and the weak chin, standing just behind her. He's Fielding's joint Managing Director.'

'*Two* managing directors?' Tay had tried not to smile at Michael Burk's cruelly accurate description of Lance Poulton. 'With only a total of four on their Board, isn't that a bit top-heavy?'

'It is,' Burke had replied with emphasis. 'But

according to the grapevine, Sven Diamond—he's the other M.D.—dictated his own terms when he joined them. Scott Fielding's a tough nut to crack, but he met his match there. Diamond's got a brilliant brain, and the only way Fielding could induce him to join their Board was to give him parity of power with Lance, and let the two of them slog it out for top spot themselves. He's keeping them from each other's throats at the moment by giving Diamond the engineering side of things, and putting Lance in charge of Sales. It'll be interesting to see which one comes out on top eventually,' he had said with ghoulish relish. 'My bet's on Diamond.'

'Which one is he?' Tay had felt a sudden curiosity to see this man who could command such respect from her dinner partner, who was himself head of his own firm, and widely known for being hard-headed and ruthless when it came to a business deal.

'I can't see Diamond at the moment,' Burk had said. 'I'll point him out to you when I spot him. Fieldings have certainly mustered their strength here tonight.'

'A gathering of eagles, in fact,' Tay had quipped.

'A gathering of vultures, more likely,' her partner had returned. 'I wonder whose bones they're hoping to pick.'

'It certainly won't be ours,' Tay had laughed confidently. 'Vultures only eat carrion. Hilliard Engineering doesn't qualify, thank goodness. Our firm's very much alive and kicking.'

She was to remember her words with bitter clarity soon afterwards.

'Here's Diamond now.' Her companion had called her attention to a man who was threading his way through the crowded room, making in the direction of their corner.

'It looks as if he's coming towards us. Is he gunning for you, or for me, do you think?' Burk had given Tay a lopsided grin.

'It must be you. He doesn't know me,' Tay had teased, and felt a curious sense of relief at the knowledge as she watched the man approaching them.

He was tall, unusually so, probably six feet two or three, she had estimated. But it was his presence rather than his height that had made him stand out.

The formal black and white of his evening attire had fitted his broad shoulders like a glove, and Tay had deduced shrewdly that the perfect tailoring had its origins in Savile Row.

She had noticed both men's and women's heads turn surreptitiously to watch him pass, but he had looked neither to left nor to right to greet anyone, as if he had a particular purpose in crossing the room, and headed single-mindedly to carry it out.

Sven Diamond.

In spite of his first name, he did not look Scandinavian. Tay had studied him as he approached. His face was strong, arresting, as well as handsome, and its features, once seen, were unlikely to be forgotten.

It was the face of a man who would not suffer fools gladly.

Tay had thought, my description fits him best. The other Fielding directors might be vultures, but this man who approached them was an eagle. A proud, strong, invincible king of birds. And when he stooped, the prey he set his heart on would have no opportunity to escape.

'Hello, Michael. How's business?' The newcomer was upon them, shaking hands with her partner, and subconsciously Tay had noted that his deep, well modulated voice held no trace of an accent. It was as English as her own.

And then she had found her hand encased in a hard grip, and Sven Diamond's eyes, incredibly blue, were fixed upon her face.

Instead of releasing her hand, Sven Diamond had

retained it in his grasp, and drawn Tay away from her companion, inviting her—no, telling her, she realised vexedly—to 'Come and meet the other members of my Board.'

Tay had not wanted to go with him, but with his hand now firmly clamped round her arm she could not help herself. The man both attracted and repelled her, and she did not want to go with Lance Poulton's formidable opposite number to meet anyone. Glancing up into the stern lines of his face, she had felt a quick sympathy for the unknown Lance.

If she was in the habit of betting, her money would be on Sven Diamond, too.

'I'm with Michael Burk,' she had protested.

'You *were* with Burk,' Sven Diamond had corrected her. 'Now, you're with me.' He had ignored Tay's outraged gasp, and gone on coolly, 'I've been watching Burk bore you to tears for the last hour. You were just begging to be rescued from him. You're worthy of better company, Copper.'

'And that's you, I suppose?' Tay had flared. 'And don't call me Copper.'

'Doesn't everybody?' he had taunted.

Everybody did, and Tay hated it. And Sven Diamond, for guessing it, and using the detested name to needle her.

'Hello, Tay,' someone had called out as they passed, and Tay had smiled automatically and called back, 'Hello,' without seeing who it was she spoke to. The smile had revealed her tiny, even teeth, and her lips had still been softly curved as she turned her head back, and unconsciously looked up into her unwelcome escort's face.

Sven Diamong had smiled back.

The lazy uptilting of his firm lips had sent an odd sensation tingling right through Tay. His smile was somehow unexpected. There was no real reason why it should be. She was accustomed to having men smile at her, even men as attractive as Sven Diamond. It was the normal response of any warm-blooded male from nineteen to ninety, when confronted by her delicate loveliness.

This man was different.

Tay had the feeling that he did not readily dispense smiles, that her own dainty looks were not the cause of this one. Perhaps, like herself, he was merely responding mechanically to the obligations of the social evening.

'Let me get you a drink, before you meet the others,' he had said.

It was a natural thing to offer her, so why did the innocent words seem to take on a sinister meaning, coming from him?

'I'm not thirsty,' Tay had begun, and felt she would much rather return to the company of the innocuous Michael Burk.

Why had her arm tingled to Sven Diamond's touch, as if she had leaned on a live electric wire? She had resisted an almost irrepressible impulse to rub it, as he ordered drinks for them both, disregarding her refusal.

'This'll keep the cold out until you reach home,' he had said, handing her a glass.

Tay had not been able to refuse it without making a fuss, although once in her hands she had felt an angry desire to hurl the glass of unwanted liquid at him, and choked as the wine stung her throat.

'Cough up, Copper.'

The flat of Sven Diamond's hand had come down smartly between Tay's shoulder blades, and she had gasped in air, and hissed at him furiously,

'If you do that again, I'll slap you right back!'

'I couldn't let you expire at my feet.'

He had sounded as if he did not care if she expired somewhere else, less inconvenient to himself, and Tay

had glared at him as he led her across to Scott Fielding
and his companions.

'I believe you already know Scott and Mrs Fielding,'
he had said, and added with a deliberate glance at his
Chairman, 'Miss Hilliard and I are already on excellent
terms.'

On such a short acquaintance, it was an odd thing to
say. Perhaps Sven Diamond was foreign, after all, in
spite of his flawless English?

Tay had smiled at Louise Fielding and her husband,
and turned to meet the other members of their Board.

Olive Poulton's scarlet fingertips touched Tay's hand
in the briefest possible handshake, and the girl's black
eyes had given her a sly look, that seemed to be secretly
laughing at her, as Tay turned to meet Lance Poulton,
who had a handshake to match his chin, and then
Andrew Gleeson.

'Miss Hilliard.' The Financial Director's narrow head
had inclined. Like a mandarin, Tay thought, with an
inward shiver as he spoke her name in a smooth,
expressionless voice, dropping the syllables like formless
spots of grease, and Tay had loosened his cold, limp hand
with almost indecent haste.

A wave of pure relief had washed over her when her
father's voice called out from behind her,

'There you are, Tay. I've been looking all over for you.
It's time we started for home, my dear.'

'What, so soon?' Olive Poulton's voice had been a
sneer. 'The night's only just started.'

'Even for you hardy Southerners, one o'clock in the
morning must see the night well on its way,' Morgan
Hilliard had replied. 'Tay and I have got a long journey
ahead of us. I fancy you'll reach your beds long before we
do.'

'Surely you can afford to put up at an hotel in Town for
just one night?' the girl had responded, with such

calculated rudeness that two spots of angry colour flagged Tay's cheeks, but before she could say anything, her father had answered with deflating calmness,

'We could, Mrs Poulton, but I don't choose to. I prefer to be back home for when the works open up in the morning. Ken Wallace, my Workshop Superintendent, is a good man, but I always say a ship sails best when the master's at the helm.'

'I'll go and collect my things,' Tay had said quickly. With a brief, 'Good night,' which included them all, she had headed for the cloakroom, with Olive Poulton's sarcastic, 'Such a *docile* daughter!' making her ears burn.

Sven Diamond had come to the hotel forecourt to see them off.

'Have a safe journey, Hilliard.' He had shaken hands briskly with her father, and then turned to Tay. 'Au revoir, Miss Hilliard.' He had bowed low over her hand, his eyes glinting mockingly into her own.

'*Goodbye*, Mr Diamond,' Tay had returned with cutting emphasis, and dropped hurriedly into the car beside her father.

'I could do without the Fielding crowd. Particularly Olive Poulton,' she had said feelingly as they cruised along the near deserted motorway.

'We shan't be able to do without them, unfortunately,' her father had replied in a studiedly careful voice, and had dropped his bombshell.

'We can't accept financial backing from Fieldings,' Tay protested. 'They're an impossible crowd. Surely there are others? What about Michael Burk?'

'Plenty of others are ready to offer sympathy, but only Fieldings have come up with any concrete proposals.'

'No, to whatever they are,' Tay cried. 'If we need money that badly, I'd rather raise a mortgage on Cloisters first.'

To Tay it was the ultimate sacrifice, and underlined

her opinion of the Fielding Board. She loved the sprawling old manor house that had sheltered generations of Hilliards, and she could not contemplate life without its always being there in the background.

'I already have,' her father answered quietly.

'You . . . already . . . *have*?' echoed Tay, in a strained whisper.

'It was the only way to keep the firm afloat.' Morgan Hilliard defended the indefensible.

Tay looked across at her father perplexedly. 'If you've mortgaged Cloisters, surely we should have enough money to carry us into production of the new model?'

'The money it raised paid for tooling up the engine. I thought it would pay for the body-tooling as well, but . . .'

But Morgan Hilliard was a perfectionist. To him, finance was a necessary evil. Tay had no difficulty in filling in the rest of his explanation unheard. It was this very perfectionism that made their hand-built cars the sought-after masterpieces they were. But with no money left for tooling up the new car body, the new engine was useless without it.

'Couldn't we put the engine under wraps, and carry on as we are with the old model, until we've straightened out financially?' she suggested.

'That might have been possible a few years ago, but not now.' Morgan Hilliard shook his head. 'With the shrinking market because of the recession, it might be some time before we're in a position to finance ourselves with new tooling for the car body, and by then the opposition could well have overtaken us with engine design. To make the impact that's necessary to recoup our investment, and put us on our feet again, we need to launch the engine now. Right away.'

Which left Scott Fielding's proposals, whatever they might be. Tay settled down to listen, feeling as if the very fabric of their lives was crumbling round her.

Her father explained, 'Fieldings have produced a new camper, which they want to launch at the African Motor Trials.'

He mentioned the international, rally-type competition that held much prestige, and offered world-wide publicity for the winner, and was an ideal venue at which to launch a brand new model. He went on,

'Their new camper's a go-anywhere vehicle, designed for rough, off-the-road use, such as safaris and so on, and the Trials would be an ideal launching-pad for it. But they need a new engine to power it, that's geared for four-wheel drive, and is bigger than anything they themselves have used in any of their leisure vehicles before. Their own design has hit snags, and it's still on the drawing board. It won't be possible for them to have it ready, and tested, in time. Our engine seems ideal for their purpose, and it's ready now.'

'We've never sold our engines separately before,' protested Tay. 'Our cars have always been exclusively Hilliards, the power-units included.'

'Times have changed, and we've got to change with them. If marketing our engines separately means saving the firm . . .' Her father left the rest of his sentence unsaid.

'If you're absolutely certain that's our only way out,' Tay agreed reluctantly. 'How many engines will Fieldings want initially?'

'Initially, they want a merger between our two companies.'

'*What?*' She sat bolt upright in her seat, and stared in disbelief at her father. 'It's unthinkable!' she cried. 'You can't—you simply *can't*—let us merge with another firm. Particularly Fieldings. They're vast—they'd swallow us whole!'

'I don't want to merge, but unless we can find some

way of riding the storm, we might have no alternative.'

Tay said in a tight voice, 'There is a way. I'll sell Mother's jewellery.'

'*No*, Tay.' Her father's reaction was violent. 'I won't countenance it,' he declared.

'But . . .'

'I said *no*, Tay,' Morgan Hilliard repeated, in a tone that allowed no appeal. 'The jewellery belongs to you. It's got nothing to do with the firm. And if Hilliards goes broke, it'll be all you'll have. I won't hear of your selling it. Please don't mention it again.'

Which closed the only avenue open to her. 'Why can't Fieldings buy our engines as ordinary customers, without merging the two companies?' she wanted to know mutinously.

'It isn't so simple as that. If their new camper happens to do well in the African Trials, they could be faced with an explosion of orders that might run into thousands. To supply them with that many engines at the rate they would want them, we'd have to expand quickly. And we haven't got the money,' he finished simply.

They were back to square one.

'Surely we can compromise, and collaborate with them, instead of merging?' Tay persisted. 'If we merge, we'll be lost for ever, whereas if we only collaborate, we can withdraw when we're on our own feet again financially, and still keep Fieldings as a customer. How did you leave it with Scott?'

'He's sending one of the Fielding Board to look over our works, to assess our potential, and look at the engine for himself. And then we'll meet at Fieldings for exploratory talks afterwards.'

Sven Diamond came.

Tay thought, this is why he said, au revoir, instead of goodbye, when he saw us off from the hotel after the

Federation Dinner. He knew, as she did not, that he would be seeing her again soon.

It was all horribly clear now.

Tay felt as if she wanted to scream her rage at Scott Fielding for being the one to make such an approach to her father, whatever their joint needs might be. And she knew, frustratedly, that if she gave vent to the storm of anger and bewilderment and shock that boiled inside her like a volcano about to erupt, ever since her father had told her the news, it would not make the slightest difference to the situation as it stood.

And now Sven Diamond was coming to assess the potential of their plant. Like a buyer at a cattle market, Tay likened him resentfully.

He arrived early.

'He'll be here by late afternoon,' Morgan Hilliard told her, preparing to depart on his morning visit to a component supplier. 'Sven's got a luncheon appointment first, and he's coming on to us from there. I'll be back before he gets here.'

'Thank goodness for that,' muttered Tay, and determined to make herself scarce when that time arrived.

In an effort to forget the impending visit, she flung herself into the morning's routine with more than her usual concentration, and by coffee-time the post was dealt with and neatly filed away, and Ken Wallace, the Workshop Superindent, popped his head round the office door with the day's routine engine-test results.

'Come and have a listen to the one on the test-bed, Miss Tay, before I switch it off,' he invited. 'It's running as smoothly as a space rocket.'

'Let's hope it doesn't develop the same characteristics,' Tay responded, but nothing loth she quickly donned the pair of dark blue dungarees hung in the office cupboard for her use, and stuck the matching peaked cap at a jaunty angle over her auburn curls. She followed the

Workshop Superintendent to the large shed, where a gleaming new engine lay on a test-bed near to the entrance door.

'Ken, there's a load of tyres just arrived. Can you come for a minute?' a voice called from the loading-bay outside.

'Carry on.' Tay released the man. 'I'll stay with the engine for a while, and gloat,' she smiled, and hoped privately that the powerful purr that emanated from her father's latest brain-child would be successful in drowning out her own unwelcome thoughts of their impending visitor.

She bent over the guard-rail that surrounded the test-bed, her eyes flickering from the meter readings to the sheet of figures in her hand, noting with satisfaction the consistent results that had not deviated now with any of their first batch of engines, through weeks of rigorous testing.

Reluctant to return to the office, she reached for a pair of ear-muffs hanging on a nearby hook, and slipped them over her head, and turned up the power until the purr became a roar, her whole mind intent on the readings in front of her.

'Boy! Where can I find Morgan Hilliard?'

A large hand landed with stinging accuracy on the tightly stretched seat of Tay's overalls, while the fingers of another tugged imperiously at the left ear-muff, moving it far enough away from the orifice it protected to enable the hand's owner to yell his question into her startled ear.

'Ouch!' Tay spun round, her hand nursing her smarting posterior. 'What are you doing here?' she exclaimed. 'You're not expected until this afternoon.'

The roar of the engine drowned her voice, and furiously she jabbed at the power switch, reducing the roar to silence. At the same time, she yanked off her ear-

muffs, dislodging her cap in the process, which fell to the
ground at her feet, and left curls revealed.

'Well, well, if it isn't Copper herself,' Sven Diamond
drawled.

'How dare you!' Tay choked.

'Belt you across your backside? Sorry about that.' His
grin looked the reverse of sorrowful, and she glowered as
he went on, 'You can hardly blame me for mistaking you
for a workshop apprentice, dressed in that rigout. You
don't look much like the girl I met at the Federation
Dinner.'

'What are you doing here so soon?' she demanded. 'If
you came early, hoping to catch us unawares . . .'

'I seem to have succeeded remarkably well,' he
observed, 'but in fact the reason I'm early isn't nearly so
sinister. My luncheon appointment was cancelled at the
last minute, and it seemed sensible to use the time taking
a more thorough look round your works, and inspecting
your engine.'

'Dad's out until after lunch.'

Which left herself in sole charge, Tay realised,
appalled.

In her father's absence, Tay normally shouldered the
duties of a guide without any qualms. But with this
particular visitor she not only had qualms but a strong,
butterflies-in-the stomach sensation that she found
highly disconcerting.

'Dad's arranged to show you round the works himself,
when he gets back this afternoon.' Desperately, she
hoped that Scott Fielding's unwelcome deputy would
have the grace to remove himself until that time arrived.

'You'll do very nicely instead,' their visitor responded
unperturbed, and Tay's lips compressed.

'I'll have to take off my overalls first.'

'I can wait.'

Defeated, Tay turned on her heel, and made for the office, Sven Diamond following.

She pushed open the door and started to struggle out of her protective clothing. She tugged at the buttons with fingers that fumbled, because Sven Diamond was watching her, and furious with herself for not appearing cool, and calm, and sophisticated, as doubtless Olive Poulton would under such circumstances.

The tiny office seemed smaller than ever, with this man inside it. He seemed to fill every available corner with his presence, making the confined space suddenly claustrophobic. With a strangled, 'Follow me,' Tay escaped through the door ahead of him.

'Gladly,' he murmured, his blue eyes raking over her trim figure with a look that brought a tide of hot colour rushing to her cheeks, and made her limbs feel stiff and jerky as she walked ahead of him through the workshops, trying without success to pretend he was just an ordinary visitor.

Desperately, she reeled off her guide's patter, convinced that he was not even listening.

His silence as he followed her from one work station to the next was unnerving, but his keen blue eyes missed nothing of what was going on around him. They seemed to be everywhere, Tay saw uneasily. Noting. Mentally recording. Criticising?

It was only when they came to the shed housing Hilliards' museum, a collection of scaled-down versions of each model the firm had produced since they first went into production, that Sven Diamond showed any sign of enthusiasm.

He walked slowly along the line of sleekly perfect model cars, each small number plate bearing its title and the year of launch.

'They're incredible,' he exclaimed. 'Do they actually work?'

'Of course.' Tay looked surprised at such a question. 'They're kept in perfect running order. I usually have the job of driving them, because I'm the only one who's small enough to get behind the steering-wheels.'

'It'd be nice to see one in action,' hinted Sven.

'We haven't got the time. There's still the new engine for you to see, yet.'

That was what he had come for, and that was what she would show him, Tay determined unhelpfully.

'Miss Tay, can you move this gentleman's vehicle round the back for a while? We've got a lorry and trailer trying to turn in the yard, and it's a tight fit. I'm afraid of the visitor's vehicle getting damaged,' an overalled figure called.

'I'll move it right away,' Tay called back. 'We're going to the engine test-shed anyhow, and it's a good walk back, so we might as well ride.' She turned to her companion. 'I'll have to drive. Outsiders aren't insured to drive on the premises, except into the car park.'

Unrepentantly, she made it plain to her visitor how she classed him.

'Will you be able to reach the pedals?' he jibed, and Tay's lips thinned as he handed over the keys, and strolled beside her to where he had parked his vehicle, well within the works perimeter, she noted vexedly, instead of in one of the slots marked for visitors.

Perhaps he did not class himself as a visitor? Perhaps, arrogantly, he already thought of himself as part owner of Hilliards?

'Is this your new camper? You've got spoilers fitted on the body.' Her trained eye detected the extra panelling, skilfully fitted to disguise the body shape from all except close scrutiny, which would effectively foil the long-range cameras of those intent upon a magazine scoop before it was launched, or, more sinisterly, industrial espionage.

'It's one of two prototypes we're trying out. This is the bigger, four-berth model. The other is a two-berth, scaled-down version. Perhaps I'd better back it away from the wall for you,' he added, giving Tay a doubtful look.

'I'm used to driving a Hilliard, so I'm quite capable of handling a production-line camper without pranging it.' With her nose in the air, she clambered up into the driving-seat, determined not to be ousted from her place at the wheel.

Sven Diamond joined her in the front, and pulled his seat-belt round him with an ostentatious attention that brought two angry spots of colour to Tay's cheeks, but she ignored him, and gave a surreptitious glance downwards at the gear stick markings.

It would be disastrous if they were a different sequence from those she was used to, and she accidentally engaged the wrong gear, and rammed the wall, confirming her arrogant passenger's worst fears as to her driving ability.

The gear meshed smoothly. The camper inched backwards in response to Tay's cautious toe on the accelerator, and with an upsurge of confidence she swung the vehicle round with a quick pull of the wheel.

'Not bad, for a woman driver,' Sven Diamond remarked loftily. 'Now let's go and see if your new engine is good enough to be fitted into our camper.'

'Whether *our engine* is good enough . . .?' Tay choked on his insolence. 'What's good enough for a Hilliard is good enough . . .'

'I rely on my own judgement,' her passenger interrupted, and Tay sucked in a difficult breath.

'And I rely on mine,' she ground out. 'If that's your attitude, then I'll find out for myself, now, whether *your* camper is fit to take *our* engine.'

Without pausing to consider the consequences of what she was doing, she slammed the camper into gear, stamped hard on the accelerator, and sent the vehicle hurtling away at top speed.

'Slow down!' her passenger shouted. 'Where do you think you're going?'

'I don't think—I know,' Tay shouted back. 'I'm taking the camper on to our test track, to see for myself if it measures up. You can see our new engine when we come back.'

If there was anything left of his vaunted camper by then, she thought grimly, and roared on.

At the speed she was going, Sven Diamond would not dare to jump out. And it would give her the greatest satisfaction to treat him to the roughest ride he had ever experienced over the specially built hazards of the Hilliards' test track.

CHAPTER TWO

A BURNING anger consumed Tay, driving her round the tight bends of the test-track at a hair-raising speed.

The camper was a much higher vehicle than the low-slung Hilliard tourer she was accustomed to, and it rocked wildly on the first hairpin bend, but with set lips she kept her foot down hard on the accelerator, extracting the maximum speed from the screaming engine.

Out of the corner of her eye, she was aware of Sven Diamond, granite-faced, and tensed back hard against his seat, his hands knuckle-white on the grab rails.

A second bend loomed up, and Tay swung into it, grinning inwardly at the fright she must be giving her passenger. She was a natural driver, and frequently tested their own cars on the track. She was familiar with every inch of it, but Sven Diamond was not to know this, and his obviously poor opinion of women drivers must be adding to his terror now.

The skid-pan lay ahead. The track widened out to allow a sliding vehicle plenty of room. A sharp scud of rain across the windscreen brought Tay's foot up instinctively off the accelerator, but she looked in vain for the instant response she was used to from the low-slung Hilliard. The much higher body of the camper made the vehicle correspondingly slower to react, and the unexpected delay took her by surprise.

The glassy surface of the skid-pan, purpose-built to make tyres lose their grip, was turned to a skating rink by the sudden shower of rain. The front tyres groped, floundered, and gave up. The back tyres did not even try.

Tay's fury evaporated with the suddenness of blowing

24

out a candle, and her mind and body froze. Her speed, when she met the skid-pan, was recklessly high. The wildly skidding wheels doubled it in as many seconds, and the vehicle spun like a top in a succession of dizzy circles. Desperately she clung to the steering-wheel, using all her strength to drive into the skids, as she had done with cool confidence hundreds of times before while testing one of their own cars.

This time, it was different. The wildly erratic movements of the camper were unpredictable and outside anything in Tay's experience. One second she needed to steer in one direction, and the next second the camper was swinging in another, and it took all the muscle power of her slender arms to pull the bucking wheel round. With a sick feeling of fear, Tay knew she had completely lost control.

Sven Diamond broke her paralysis.

'Loose the wheel!' he roared, and wrenched it from out of her grasp.

His arms came hard round her, taking control, his body half sitting, half standing, leaning against her to steady himself in the gyrating vehicle. His weight pressed against her, pushing the breath from her lungs, suffocating her.

Tay closed her eyes, and waited for the camper to roll over, trapping them both inside. Then, in a daze, it dawned upon her that the violent motion of the camper had ceased. She opened her eyes, and blinked up at the blue fury that glared back into them.

'You crazy female!' thundered Sven Diamond. 'I ought to bend you across my knee and wallop some sense into you!'

'D-don't you d-dare,' she stuttered, shrinking away from him, her eyes wide green pools in her chalk-white face.

'You might have wrecked the camper, and killed yourself!'

And him. The realisation made her heart do a flip in her breast.

'As it is, you've probably done untold damage, racing it across those pavé setts at such a crazy speed,' he snarled.

'If the design's any good, it should stand up to it,' Tay flung back, twin spots of angry colour revitalising her cheeks. 'Not that it *is* any good,' she cried scornfully. 'The beastly thing rocks like a skiff in a force 9 gale, and it takes for ever to respond to the controls.'

'The camper's not designed to be driven by a lunatic!' he shouted back. 'If it wasn't for its superb road holding, we'd have rolled right over on that first bend, the way you were driving it!'

'Scared you, did I?' jeered Tay, and caught her breath as the blue eyes turned as hard as their owner's name.

'You're the worst driver I've ever had the evil luck to ride with,' their owner grated. 'You're not fit to hold a licence!'

'Don't worry, you'll be perfectly safe on the way back. I won't drive at more than five miles an hour,' Tay taunted him.

'You won't drive another vehicle with me on board,' he growled, and then grabbed her.

With a quick twist that foiled her convulsive move to break free, he lifted her from behind the wheel, and unceremoniously bundled her into the passenger seat.

She turned on him furiously. 'You can't drive on our track,' she cried. 'I've told you. You're not insured.'

'I enjoy taking risks, Copper. Hasn't anyone told you?' Roughly he pulled her to him, and kissed her hard on the mouth, silencing her protests.

The pressure of his lips drove her head backwards, bruising her mouth. Showing her no mercy, as she had shown none to him. Punishing her for her recklessness in a way that was worse than any spanking could have been.

Fiercely Tay fought him, but his hold on her was

implacable, too tight for even her wiry strength to break free from his arms. The pressure of his lips was relentless, cutting off her breath, and dismay washed over her as she felt her senses begin to slip.

She made a small, inarticulate sound deep in her throat, and began to go limp in his arms.

Immediately his lips released her. She drew in a long, shuddering breath, but her respite lasted for only a second or two before his lips came down again, more gently this time, tantalising her mouth with a deadly expertise that demanded a response.

Tingles of awareness felt their way through her like tiny electric probes, and galvanised her into frightened life. If the camper was outside her experience, so was Sven Diamond. He was taking control of her with the same ruthless efficiency with which he took control of the camper, and she felt herself losing her grip as rapidly as the tyres lost theirs on the greasy track.

Another minute ... another second ...

Violently she pushed away from him, and after what seemed an eternity she felt his arms slacken their hold, and she lay back, panting, on her seat.

'I hate you for that!' she shrilled. Angrily she tugged a hand across her throbbing lips, desperately trying to wipe away the feel of his kiss. 'If you want that kind of entertainment, you won't find it here. I'm not part of the engine deal. You're here to look round the works, not for this.'

'What makes you so sure I didn't come for both, Copper?' he drawled, and his eyes bored into Tay's with a look that made her crouch back in her seat, as he keyed the engine into life, and drove the camper steadily back along the test-track towards the distant buildings.

Their visit to Scott Fielding's house for the subsequent talks was equally disastrous.

Immediately after Sven Diamond's visit, two of the new engines were crated and despatched for trial fitting in the prototype campers, and a week later, Tay and her father followed them.

Their visit coincided with Scott Fielding's silver wedding anniversary, and Tay and her father had been invited to remain for the weekend. Tay expressed her surprise at the invitation, commenting, 'Surely Scott Fielding won't want to hold business meetings on his wedding anniversary?'

'To men of Fielding's outlook, nothing has to stand in the way of business,' her father responded, and it was with deep misgivings that Tay watched him settle their suitcases into the boot of the Hilliard, before she joined him in the front of the car to start their journey south.

'You don't usually wear make-up,' observed Morgan Hilliard, giving her lightly lipsticked mouth, and carefully disguised freckles, a questioning look.

'This isn't make-up—it's warpaint!'

Her father smiled. 'Don't worry, love. You'll outshine Olive Poulton any day,' he comforted.

Olive Poulton was not Tay's main concern.

She blinked as she caught sight of an Olympic-sized swimming-pool and an array of rigidly netted tennis courts as they drove up the long drive to Scott Fielding's house. The car swung to a halt on smooth tarmac beside the imposing entrance, and she decanted from her seat, feeling as if she were about to enter a multi-star hotel.

Compared to the welcoming, age-weathered sprawl of Cloisters the Fielding residence was large, angular, and aggressively modern. The inside appearance of the house bore out Tay's first impression. A smart maid answered their ring and guided them through a featureless hall into an imposing drawing-room that had been furnished regardless of cost, and succeeded only in looking as if it were a commissioned interior from the pages of a glossy magazine.

It was the house of a man to whom success meant only one thing—wealth, and who was determined that his lifestyle should proclaim that success to the world.

Scott Fielding's welcome was cordial enough, however.

'Come and have tea.' He drew them into the drawing-room, where his wife and the three other members of his Board were already foregathered. Olive, Tay saw alertly, was not present. Had she deliberately opted out, as a slight to themselves?

Lance said, in half-apology for his wife's absence, as he shook hands, 'Olive will be down in a moment. She's just finishing doing her hair.'

'My wife and Olive will entertain Tay, while we take her father round the works,' Scott told the room at large, and Tay wondered how Olive Poulton would react to their host's disposal of her time. She was under no illusion that any hospitality extended by Olive would be under duress and not voluntary.

The other girl ought to thank her for disposing of her difficulty, she thought, as she said aloud, 'Oh, but I'll be coming with you on the tour. I want to see over your factory for myself.'

Her host smiled, but she noticed that it was a movement of his lips only, and did nothing to warm the cold grey eyes that summed her up. Tay thought, they're as expressionless as the eyes of a poker player.

'Come now, a noisy engineering works can't hold anything of interest to a young lady like yourself,' he said, in a jocular tone that did not quite succeed in hiding his irritation at Tay's lack of co-operation.

She eyed him calmly. 'On the contrary,' she replied, 'it holds a great deal of interest for me. And so do the coming talks between us.'

She made it clear that she intended to participate in the talks as well, and Scott Fielding's face lost its smile as she went on evenly, 'I play an active part in the running of our own plant.'

The silence in the room was complete. Teacups

stopped clinking, and Tay felt six pairs of eyes focused on her. In particular, one pair of intensely blue eyes. She wondered what their owner thought of her passage-at-arms with his Chairman. She did not care.

'In a small plant like your own, that may be permissible,' Scott Fielding allowed, and Tay cut in,

'I don't need anyone's permission. I hold half of my mother's shares in the firm, which gives me the right to a share in any decision that affects its future. I'm not merely a sleeping partner, Mr Fielding.'

As she spoke the words, for some reason her eyes found Sven's face, and the words she had flung at him on the test-track flashed across her mind.

'If you want that kind of entertainment, you won't find it here . . .'

The amusement in his blue eyes told her that he remembered it, too, and deliberately misinterpreted her words, 'I'm not merely a sleeping partner,' and gave them a meaning wholly his own.

She felt hot colour rush up her throat and cheeks, and turned gratefully to her hostess as Louise Fielding said,

'Are you sure you wouldn't prefer to stay here with me, and have your tea in peace, my dear? I'm afraid my husband doesn't approve of women in business. Olive wanted shares, when Lance joined the firm, but Scott was quite adamant. Olive will be here in a moment, I'm sure,' she added as further inducement.

At that moment, Olive Poulton walked into the room. To be more accurate she made an entrance.

She was dressed to startle. Her bright scarlet shift was deceptively simple in style and cut, and was the kind of dress that cost the earth in a Paris salon. Tay felt convinced that Olive had chosen to wear it this afternoon deliberately to outclass her own outfit, and felt uncharitably pleased that the other girl's manoeuvre did not succeed.

If Olive had left her hair to its own natural darkness, to

match her sultry black eyes, the effect would have been stunning. As it was, under her peroxide blonde mane, the dress looked merely garish.

The girl drifted languidly towards the tea trolley, murmuring a vague 'Hello, everybody.'

She ignored her husband, gave Sven a long look from under her heavily mascaraed eyelashes, and getting no response, pouted in a petulant manner, and turned her attention to the tea-trolley.

'If you've finished your tea, Morgan, shall we start our tour of the works?' asked Scott, into the uncomfortable silence that followed Olive's entrance.

He pointedly did not include Tay in the invitation, and with tight lips she put down her half-finished cup of tea and glued herself to her father's side as he walked out of the room with his host, followed by Lance, Andrew Gleeson, and Sven. Like a guard of honour, she thought, with a sudden urge to giggle.

Or a posse of jailers. The desire to giggle vanished.

To her relief, Olive did not accompany them, but her vitriolic glare followed Tay to the door, indicative of her resentment that she herself was barred from the proceedings.

The next two hours was an education for Tay.

Accustomed as she was to the slow pace of their own hand-crafted car manufacture, turning out vehicles at the rate of a mere handful a week, the sight of the robot machinery churning out components at bewildering speed left her feeling slightly dizzy.

It did not help that she found herself sandwiched between Lance and Sven in the open golf buggy that took them on the tour. Andrew Gleeson drove the first buggy, with her father and Scott Fielding, and Sven drove the second one.

He explained their transport off-handedly as, 'Another of our products. They sell very well, world-wide.'

'Perhaps you'd like a turn at the wheel on the way back?' Lance offered.

'You won't drive another vehicle, with me on board.' No sound came from Sven's mouth, but his oblique look repeated his earlier words, and Tay stiffened.

Sven would make very sure she had no opportunity to drive the buggy. And perversely, it immediately became her ambition. The buggies were fun to ride in. They would be even more fun to drive.

When the works tour was over, and they were all seated together at dinner that evening, Andrew Gleeson suggested, 'If you expanded, Morgan, you could put in robots yourself, and treble your production without increasing your work force.'

He still wore his tinted spectacles, even inside the house, and Tay wondered sourly if they affected the colour of his cabbage. Her nerves tingled as she waited for her father's answer.

'I can't afford to install robot machinery.'

'We'll fund you, of course, initially.' Scott Fielding offered. 'After all, we should absorb your entire output of engines, except for the few you'd need for your own vehicles.'

He said it with barely disguised contempt, dismissing their own comparatively small production as a mere sideline, and as if it were a foregone conclusion that Morgan Hilliard would fall in with the suggestions of a company as large as his own, without question.

'I'll consider what you say,' her father replied, and Tay turned to him, aghast.

'We can't possibly consider such a thing.' She dismissed the suggestion out of hand. 'If we put ourselves into debt to that extent, and Fieldings cancel their order for our engines, we'd be ruined, and then . . .'

And then, Fieldings could take over Hilliard Engineering lock, stock and barrel, on whatever terms they chose. Tay felt the atmosphere in the room grow electric at her outspoken opposition, and Scott's face glowered at her from the top of the table.

'There are signed agreements to prevent such a thing happening, Tay,' her father pointed out.

'There's such a thing as petticoat government, too,' murmured Olive in a snide aside that was deliberately calculated to inflame Scott's prejudices on that particular score.

Tay's breath hissed through clenched teeth. 'The risk's all on our side, just the same,' she insisted, ignoring Olive.

'In business, you have to be prepared to take risks. Financial, and otherwise,' Sven put in, and Tay looked across the table at him, startled.

What did he mean, by 'and otherwise'?

On his own admission, he enjoyed taking risks. But the circumstances under which he confessed to his predilection could hardly be described as commercial, she remembered uncomfortably. And his reaction to it definitely did not come under that category. Perhaps that was what he meant by 'and otherwise.'

Her cheeks warmed at the thought, and Sven's eyes mocked her from his seat across the table, enigmatic pools of blue that for some reason Tay found suddenly difficult to meet.

Lance defused the atmosphere while coffee was being served in the drawing-room afterwards. He produced a large folder of close-up photographs of the new Fielding camper, and passed them on to the visitors to look at.

'Are these press photographs?' asked Morgan Hilliard, flicking through them, and passing them on to Tay to look at.

'Heaven forbid!' Lance exclaimed. 'The camper's still on the secret list, so far as the press is concerned. Although I've no doubt several of the motoring correspondents would give their right arms to get a sight of these pictures.'

'Which version of the camper do you intend to enter
for the African Motor Trials?' Morgan Hilliard held up
one of the photographs, which showed the two vehicles
parked side by side. 'In outward appearance, there seems
little difference between the two.'

'The four-berth version will compete.' Lance answered. 'The two-berth camper will be used as the back-
up vehicle, carrying spares and so on. Our entry, of
course, will depend upon our finding a suitable engine.
From Sven's report on his visit to your factory, your
engine is a superb power-unit.'

'Naturally. It's a Hilliard,' murmured Tay, and won a
quick grin from Lance.

He was the most human member of the Fielding
Board, she decided, and from Scott's frown, currently in
his Chairman's bad books for uttering words of approval
that might give Morgan Hilliard an inflated idea of what
his new engine might be worth to Fieldings. Olive was
scowling at her husband too, Tay noticed.

'The two versions of the camper have a similar body,'
Sven cut in. 'The only difference is that the four-berth
vehicle has a slightly longer wheelbase to accommodate
extra storage-space for the double passenger load. It's
only a few inches longer, which is why it's difficult to tell
the two vehicles apart, unless they're actually parked side
by side, as they are in that photograph.'

'Let me see.' Tay turned to take the photograph from
her father. 'Oh, hold on to it for a second or two. I've
slopped my coffee in the saucer. I'll wipe my fingers
before I touch the photograph.

She snapped open her handbag standing beside her
chair, and taking out her handkerchief she wiped her
fingers free from coffee splashes before she took the
photograph from her father, and studied it carefully.

'Are you satisfied now that our camper's fit to take
your engine?' Sven jibed, coming to stand behind her
chair.

She shot him a hostile look. 'I'll let you know when I
see how your vehicle performs at the Trials.'

'A vehicle's only as good as its power-unit,' he
observed, and Tay glared, and tapped the handful of
photographs together with sharp fingers before holding
out her hand to give them back to Lance.

In doing so, a corner of the pack caught against
Andrew Gleeson's sleeve and spilled the pasteboards
across the carpet, and with a muttered apology Tay bent
to pick them up, thankful for the excuse to present her
back to Sven.

'I think that's the lot.' She straightened up, and
shuffled the pack back into order again. 'Oh, no, Mr
Gleeson's picked up some as well.' She handed over the
ones she had retrieved, and thankfully followed her
father out of the room as he made his excuses, and
withdrew.

'I think I'll turn in, now. It's been a long day.' He
nodded good night, and then kissed Tay on her cheek as
they reached the upper landing together, and she turned
towards the door of her room.

'Did you know your handbag's open, love?' her father
asked her, and she looked down at it, surprised.

'So it is, I remember, I opened it when I got my hanky
out, to wipe my fingers. I thought I'd shut it again, but I
couldn't have done. My hanky's not here—it must have
dropped out in the drawing-room. I'll go back downstairs
and pick it up, or the maid will wonder who it belongs to
when she comes to do the clearing up.'

She turned and ran lightly downstairs again and
crossed the hall towards the drawing-room, and paused
outside the door as Scott Fielding's harsh voice reached
her through the crack where it was not completely closed.

'I can handle Hilliard,' he was saying. 'It's up to you to
take on the girl, Diamond. She's fighting for collaboration. She's dead against the idea of a merger. Change her
mind for her, and do it fast. I don't care what methods

you use. Make her fall in love with you. She'll be like putty in your hands then, and she'll do anything you tell her. Compromise her, if you like. But move quickly, before anyone else has a chance to get in ahead of us.'

'I'll change her mind for her, don't worry,' Sven's voice promised, and Tay thought furiously, you will, will you? We'll see about that, Sven Diamond!

'Make sure you succeed, and don't be too long about it,' his Chairman ordered. 'That new engine of Hilliard's is revolutionary. If we can push a merger through quickly, we stand to clean up a fortune on royalties, and leave Hilliard to bear all the production costs. I want his signature safely on the bottom af an agreement, so that he can't back out. All these brilliant designers are dreamers. I doubt if he'll even notice how I word the agreement until it's too late. But the girl's a stumbling block—she's suspicious. And she's the type who'll read the small print.'

'Morgan Hilliard's no fool, Scott,' Sven's voice warned.

'You'll discover I'm no fool either!' fumed Tay.

It took all her self-control not to burst into the room and roundly condemn her host and his Board there and then, but Olive's voice stopped her.

'All this talk about engines bores me. I'm going to bed,' the girl's sulky tones declared, and Tay's feet took wings. It would be disastrous if she were caught eavesdropping.

She took to her heels and fled back up the stairs and her heart hammered as the crack of light through the drawing-room door widened just as she reached the wide landing, dived into the sanctuary of her bedroom, and pushed the door to behind her, leaving only a slight crack through which she heard Olive call,

'Good night, everybody.' And then, more loudly as the drawing-room door opened wider to allow the girl through into the hall, 'Are you coming up, Lance? Or are you going to stay downstairs half the night, as usual, talking business?'

She had not been detected.

Tay closed the door quickly, and switched on the light, and there was a smile on her face as she began slowly to undress.

Scott Fielding would find it more difficult then he imagined to manipulate her father, particularly after what she would have to tell Morgan Hilliard in the morning about the conversation she had just overheard.

As for Sven ...

'Use any method you like,' Scott Fielding had instructed him.

Which gave him plenty of leeway, but whichever method Sven might choose, Tay promised herself grimly, he would find that two could play at that particular game.

'Fighting dirty, is he?' Morgan Hilliard said thoughtfully the next morning, when Tay recounted what she had heard. 'I'll make him pay for that.'

In the meeting that followed between them, he made Scott Fielding pay, with interest.

What started as an amicable discussion between the two sides rapidly became a verbal battle ground, and Scott's chagrin knew no bounds when he discovered to his cost that the unrealistic dreamer he supposed Morgan Hilliard to be turned into a canny Northerner with an even sharper head for a business deal than he possessed himself.

Without revealing the cause of the anger that motivated him, Tay's father drove a bargain so hard that it made her gasp.

Part of the price for the use of engines in the Fielding campers at the African Trials was to take Ken Wallace as co-driver on the competing vehicle, which Sven himself was to drive. Tay was to accompany the Fielding mechanic in the back-up camper, and all expenses were to be paid by Fieldings.

Morgan Hilliard himself was to be provided with a suite of offices at the Fielding dealers in Nairobi, where the two campers were to be on display for a week before the Trials began.

'Why should Tay go with you?' complained Olive. 'You don't take me when you go abroad. Why should she walk in, and straight away get taken on a trip to Kenya?'

'Oh, all right, if you're going to whine about it, I'll take you, otherwise I suppose I'll never hear the last of it.' Impatiently Lance cut short her complaining. 'But Tay's only going there to work.' He explained the terms of the deal in a way which made it sound as if Tay was going to don overalls and wield a spanner.

'Have fun,' sneered Olive, in a tone that hoped it would be no fun at all for Tay.

Any discussion on a possible merger, or even collaboration between the two companies, had been firmly set aside by Morgan Hilliard until after the Trials were over, and since it was impossible to hold any talks without him, Scott Fielding had no option but to submit, which he did with a decidedly ill grace, Tay saw with an inward grin.

'Clean bowled!' she crowed when she was able to speak to her father alone.

'The innings isn't finished yet,' he cautioned. 'It's four against two. And now they're aware we're not going to be such easy prey as they imagined, they'll hunt us with that much more cunning.'

'We've won the first round, though,' Tay gloated. 'They can't launch their camper without us.'

'They also know that we can't launch our engine without financial backing,' her father reminded her. 'So don't get too cock-a-hoop. The game isn't over yet.'

Sven would find her a worthy opponent, Tay determined, as she joined the throng at the wedding anniversary party that evening.

Most of the guests seemed to be senior managers and

their wives from the Fielding factory. Tay wondered if Scott had any real friends whom he could invite. The conversation of the men appeared to be almost exclusively shop, and Tay felt chilled by the atmosphere of artificial bonhomie that was as brittle as the fine, hand-cut crystal glasses in which the wine was served.

Scott and his fellow directors circulated among the guests, dancing dutifuly with each of the women in turn, while Morgan Hilliard waltzed with their hostess.

Tay endured a dance with Andrew Gleeson. His dancing was as cold and stiff as the man himself, and she felt as if she were dancing with an icicle.

Deliberately she avoided meeting Sven's eye.

She determined to make it as difficult for him as she possibly could to carry out Scott's outrageous instruction of the night before.

Let him dance with Olive, she told herself unrepentantly. Olive sat twiddling her wine glass between a finger and thumb, a look of unutterable boredom on her face. Her expression did not lighten even when Lance took her on to the floor, although she responded with swift animation when Sven asked her to dance, Tay noticed, and wondered if her husband noticed the sudden change, too, and if so, what he thought of it.

She was engaged in the unsatisfactory pursuit of trying to answer her own questions, when the music struck up again, and Sven began to thread his way towards her.

Swiftly, she escaped into the more-than-willing arms of one of the younger managers, who introduced himself at Paul, and to his delight she remained with him for the next two dances.

He wrongly imagined Tay's willingness to continue dancing with him to stem from his own irresistable attraction, and by the third dance he assumed an air of jaunty proprietorship which Tay found both amusing and irritating.

Scott Fielding himself put an end to his self-

satisfaction, and in the face of such opposition the young
man ignominiously fled and left Tay to the mercy of his
Chairman. Tay tensed, but before Scott had half circled
the floor he said apologetically,

'I see my wife's signalling me. I'd better go and see
what she wants, in case some minor crisis has cropped
up.'

His smile dismissed such an absurd possibility in his
well run household, and broadened as he drew to a halt
beside Sven, and remarked as if the thought had just
occurred to him, 'I'll hand you over to Sven to look after.
I'm sure he's a much better dancer than I am.'

It was adroitly managed, and Tay was helpless to do
anything about it. Scott delivered her right into Sven's
waiting arms. Like a parcel, she thought angrily, and
caught her host's glance at Sven that clearly said, 'It's up
to you, now, to deliver.'

If she had not overheard Scott's orders the night
before, she would probably not have read any signifi-
cance into the look. Now it screamed collusion. Tay's
chin tilted defiantly. Whatever Sven had in mind, he
would discover that she was ready for him.

She might even play along with him, for just so long as
it suited her. It might afford her some amusement to
while away the time until she and her father could
decently start for home tomorrow, she thought. And
wondered at the sudden bleakness that swept over her at
the prospect of playing out the charade with Sven as her
co-actor.

Olive had obviously reckoned on claiming Sven for the
next dance, and her black eyes glittered angrily as Sven
said to her,

'Here comes Lance, to claim your next dance.'

Sven put his arms round Tay with a formal 'Shall we?'
which was totally unnecessary, since his hands were
already linked behind her, preventing her from any
attempt at escape, as he danced her on to the floor, and

round the room under Scott Fielding's observant eye.

To prove he was carrying out his boss's instructions, Tay thought with cynical contempt, and tensed as, instead of continuing on a second circuit of the room, he danced her through the open french windows on to the dusky coolness of the terrace outside. He stopped beside the balustrade and accused her,

'Playing hard to get tonight, Copper?'

'I don't know what you mean,' Tay retorted with dignity.

'You know very well what I mean,' he said, and there was an edge to his voice.

He's bothered about getting into Scott's bad books for not dancing with me before, she thought, and smiled at the success of her strategy so far, as he went on tersely,

'If you dance with young Paul just one more time he'll consider he's got a right to stake a claim on you.'

'That's when he'll discover his mistake.'

'You're cruel.'

Not half so cruel as he was. Tay's lips twisted with unexpected bitterness. Sven was using her as a pawn in a game that had no regard for the loser, still less for her own personal feelings. If she happened to get hurt in the playing of it, that would be just too bad as far as her opponent was concerned.

'If Paul gets the wrong idea, it's not my fault.'

'You can hardly blame the man. He's made of flesh and blood, not stone, and you're looking very lovely tonight, Copper.'

He was not wasting any time.

Tay forced a smile to her lips. 'I'm glad you approve of my dress,' she said demurely.

It was the palest shade of grey, with the soft, pearly lustre of a dove's wing, and relieved only by a rhinestone belt encircling her slender waist. She looked like a delicate incarnation of the twilight itself.

Suddenly, the man gave a muffled exclamation.

'Tay,' he muttered hoarsely, and took her in his arms.
His kiss was convincing.

It took all Tay's self-control not to wrench herself free,
and scream her condemnation of his infamous behaviour
in his face. But she was determined to make Sven pay for
that behaviour, as high a price as his Chairman had
already had to pay her father. And to do that, he must not
be allowed to guess that she was aware of his treachery.

By an immense effort of will she forced herself to
remain pliant in Sven's arms.

Even though she knew the reason behind his kisses, it
did not alter the electric thrill that followed the course of
his lips as they explored the soft contours of her mouth.

'You're lovely,' he murmured, and his ardour tracked
fire across her cheeks and throat, as his fingers tilted her
chin further up to tip her face towards his. The heat of his
kiss set her veins on fire, and tongues of awareness
flickered through her body with a heat that threatened to
burn her up.

If this was only play-acting on Sven's part, what would
it be like to experience the real thing? Tay wondered.

CHAPTER THREE

To Tay's surprise, Olive came down to breakfast the next morning.

The moment Tay walked unto the breakfast-room she sensed the tension in the atmosphere. After-the-party hangovers, she deduced. She would be glad to leave this house. She was tired of Olive's spite and the thinly veiled antagonism of Scott and his ménage. Sven's play-acting on the terrace last night had been the last straw, and it had left her feeling unaccountably disturbed.

Tay felt heavy-eyed and on edge as she chose her modest breakfast from the laden sideboard, and felt thankful that Sven had not yet put in an appearance. With luck, she would be long gone by the time he did.

Even Lance's cheerful face bore an expression of strain, she noticed. He strolled over to join her as she finished her single slice of toast, and said in a voice which he strove hard to make casual,

'If you've finished with the photograph you were looking at yesterday, Tay, will you let me have it back, please? I'll need it for publicity purposes for the launch in Kenya.'

Tay looked at him in surprise. 'I gave all the photographs back to you.'

'*All* of them?' Scott Fielding cut in, and his voice was curt.

'Yes, of course, all of them,' answered Tay. 'What makes you ask?'

'One of the photographs is missing from the folder,' Lance answered, and with blank astonishment Tay saw that his eyes held accusation.

'Well, I haven't got it,' she declared. 'Why should I want to keep one of your photographs?'

The atmosphere had become suddenly charged, and Sven's arrival at that moment did nothing to lighten it. He came through the door with the morning paper in his hand, and a look of thunder on his face.

Morning-after-the-party bad temper seemed to have afflicted all of them, Tay thought. But there was no need for them to take it out on her. After last night's treatment by Sven, she was the one who felt aggrieved.

'Are you sure the photograph didn't drop in your handbag? *Accidentally*, of course,' added Olive, with a thin sarcasm that sent bright flags of temper waving in Tay's cheeks. 'Your bag was open beside your chair—I saw it myself.'

'I told you, I don't have your wretched photograph,' Tay denied. 'If you don't believe me, look in my handbag for yourself. It's not there.'

Angrily, she snapped open her bag and thrust it towards Olive.

'It wouldn't be there now, would it?' sneered Olive. 'You're hardly likely to leave it in such an obvious place.' She shrugged away the bag which Lance took from Tay's hand, to pass on to his wife.

Did he do it to save Olive the trouble of stretching her arm to take it? Or to see inside its opened top for himself? Tay felt anger boil up inside her.

'I wasn't the only one who handled the photographs,' she flared. 'Mr Gleeson had some too. He helped me to pick them up from the floor when I dropped them.'

'Which gave you an ideal opportunity to slide one into your bag,' Olive suggested nastily.

'Why don't you ask Mr Gleeson? He might have it, tucked in one of his pockets somewhere,' Tay suggested, and added, 'whichever photograph it is that's missing.'

'I'm not in the habit of playing practical jokes on my fellow directors, Miss Hilliard,' the Financial Director said coldly, his dark glasses staring his disdain at such an outrageous notion.

'The photograph that's missing is the one of the two

campers parked side by side,' said Lance.

'She already knows which one's missing. She was the last one to have it in her hand,' Olive cut in spitefully.

'I haven't got it now.'

'I don't believe you.'

'I believe her. Tay hasn't got it,' said Sven, and Tay turned to him with a surge of relief. But instead of meeting the support she expected, she stared aghast at the blazing anger in his blue eyes.

'Tay hasn't got the photograph,' he reiterated. 'The Sunday newspapers have got it.'

With an angry flourish, he shook out the newspaper he carried in his hand and revealed the motoring page, which carried banner headlines.

SCOOP PREVIEW OF FIELDING'S SECRET NEW CAMPER.

'Whoever leaked that photograph to the press must have been very well paid,' Sven gritted, and Tay blanched at the blistering contempt in his voice.

'Tay wouldn't do such a thing,' Morgan Hilliard claimed. 'She may be impulsive, but she'd never be so foolish as to ...'

'The person who leaked the photograph didn't do it on a foolish impulse,' snapped Sven. 'It was a calculated, deliberate move, designed to take all the impact out of our launch at the African Trials.'

'You can't complain at the publicity you're getting now,' Tay jibed, with a derisory wave of her hand towards the headline.

'That doesn't excuse what virtually amounts to industrial espionage,' Sven snarled. 'It could land you in very serious trouble.'

'Why me? I didn't take your beastly photograph.'

'Can you prove it?'

'Of course I can't prove it. But it so happens I don't have the sort of principles that thinks any means justifies an end.'

Let him make what he liked of that. In her view,

leaking a photograph to the press was lily-white compared to what he had undertaken to do for his Chairman.

'Common sense should tell you it couldn't be me,' she rushed on. 'How could I get a photograph to a newspaper, in time for it to be printed in this morning's issue? I didn't leave the house all evening.'

'By using those big green eyes of yours to coerce one of the managers into delivering it for you, that's how,' Sven threw at her, and Tay went white. 'I saw you using them to good effect on young Paul.' His own eyes were like chips of blue ice on her face, noting her receding colour. Reading into it, what? Guilt? The scorn on his face answered her question for her. 'Paul went home early from the party.'

'And you think I gave him the photograph to deliver to the newspaper on his way?' Tay gave a high-pitched laugh. 'Your imagination's running riot! You sound like a second-rate whodunit.'

'Industrial espionage isn't something that's confined to fiction, as you should know.'

'I wouldn't demean myself by spying out your firm's secrets, let alone selling them,' she declared proudly. 'Ask Paul if I gave him the photograph. He'll soon put an end to your silly notions. Ask any of the managers. Paul couldn't have been the only one who left the party early.'

At such a party, the look in her eyes said plainly, she could not imagine any of the guests wishing to linger.

'I mean to do just that.'

'Go ahead, and good luck to your sleuthing.' Disconcertingly, Tay discovered a catch in her voice that she could not quite control. Before it could get any worse, she made her escape. 'But when I've gone,' with her hand on the door knob, her voice hardened, 'when I've gone, the person who leaked that photograph to the press will still be here. Most probably in this very room!' she shouted, and slammed the door behind her.

To Tay's relief, Sven did not fly out to Kenya with them.

'He's meeting us in Nairobi,' Lance told her, and left
Tay to wonder for the duration of the flight what his
attitude would be towards her when they met again.

'Did you find out who leaked the photograph to the
press?' Tay confronted Scott the moment they met at
Heathrow airport.

'No,' Scott admitted, 'but Sven managed to turn the
unfortunate affair to good account.' He would, Tay
thought. 'Sven entertained all the journalists from the
motoring press and gave them full details of our plans for
the Trials. With the exception of the paper that first
published the photograph, of course.'

Which told her that Sven had neither forgotten, nor
forgiven, the culprits on either side.

He was leaning negligently against the side of a mini-
bus when they emerged from Customs at Nairobi
airport. He was dressed in tropical whites, and the
casually opened neck of his shirt showed off the strong,
tanned column of his throat as he unpeeled himself off
the bus and came towards them.

'Did you have a good trip?' His enquiry was directed
impartially to anyone who cared to answer.

'The trip was. fine.' Lance replied for them all, and
Olive immediately contradicted him with a peevish, 'It
was nothing of the sort. We met a lot of turbulence. It
made me feel quite ill.'

Tay remained silent, wrestling with a sudden dryness
in her throat. She deliberately chose a seat at the rear of
the bus to be as far away as possible from Sven in the
driving-seat.

She stared fixedly out of the window as he supervised
the porter who was stowing their cases on to the roof-
rack. The engine started and she relaxed, only to spin
round, shocked, as the seat beside her subsided under
someone's weight, and Sven asked,

'Did *you* have a good trip, Copper? Or does flying
make you feel ill, too?'

'Ill' was an understatement of the way she was feeling now. The turbulence seemed to have taken possession of her stomach, giving rise to an elemental war of emotions that was frighteningly familiar from their last encounter.

The mini-bus started off with a jerk, with the man whom she supposed to be the porter at the wheel instead of Sven. Desperately, Tay tried to shrink closer to the window, away from him, and was instantly foiled by the driver.

He swung his vehicle in and out of the traffic with happy abandon, and one particularly wild swerve, to avoid a head-on collision with an oncoming taxi, tossed Tay like a cork almost on to Sven's lap. She groped wildly for a hand-hold to steady herself.

'I was fine, on the flight' she gasped, 'but I shan't be if our driver doesn't slow up. What does he think he'd doing? Practising for the Trials?'

'Hold tight, we're nearly there,' Sven assured her, and putting both his arms round her, he held her tight himself instead.

And dissolved any hope Tay might have entertained that he would abandon his obnoxious campaign to try to make her change her mind about the merger while they were in Kenya.

It was even worse that he did not seem to mind about using his tactics in public, she thought furiously. She was uncomfortably conscious of the overt glances from the others seats, but Sven seemed oblivious to her hot-cheeked embarrassment, and did not release her until the bus stopped on the forecourt of their hotel.

With a withering look that seemed to make not the slightest impression on him, Tay ejected from her seat, and out into the hot glare of the sunshine, and an equally torrid glare from Olive, who muttered furiously as she descended from the bus beside Tay,

'What do you think you're doing, fooling around like some callow teenager in the back of the cinema?'

'Having fun,' Tay flashed back. 'That's what you told me to do, wasn't it?'

And turning her back on both Olive and Sven, she made good her escape before the turbulence inside her erupted in a storm of tears that could only be caused by exhaustion from the long, ten-hour flight from England.

She managed to avoid Sven for the rest of the day. She used jet-lag as an excuse to remain in her room, but the next day was Monday, and the Trials were due to begin in the afternoon, and during the morning Tay was drawn into the maelstrom of press interviews, route briefings, and last-minute hitches, along with the rest of the competing crews.

Journalists turned up in force at the dealer's show-rooms, and photographed everything and everybody in sight who had anything to do with the Trials. The two campers stood proudly in the showroom windows, glistening with polish like two newly minted coins.

'That's funny, the campers seem to have changed places during the night,' one of the press men remarked, scratching his head with a puzzled frown. 'When I took a shot of them yesterday, I could have sworn the smaller camper was on the right. Now it's on the left, nearest the door.'

'I'll have a word with our Public Relations people, and tell them to entertain you with something a bit less potent the next time,' quipped Sven, and the man laughed, and cajoled,

'Let's have a picture of you all together, Mr Diamond. One for the front page. Come on, love, give us a smile,' he urged Tay.

It was difficult to smile, with Sven's arm lying in false camaraderie across her shoulders, but somehow Tay managed it. 'Wait a minute. I want to be in on the picture, too.' Olive pushed up to Sven, and took his arm in a proprietorial gesture, and flashed a brilliant smile in the direction of the cameras.

'If you're not in the team, you're not in the

photograph,' one of the reporters told her, with an economy of tact that brought a gasp of outrage from Olive.

'I'm the wife of a Fielding director,' she announced haughtily.

'If you're the owner himself, it'd make no difference, lady. We want pictures of the team only,' another reporter called out impatiently. 'Will you stand to one side, please, while we ...'

'Oh, keep your wretched photograph! Newspaper pictures are always awful, anyway,' Olive snapped, and flounced away, and the man grinned, and said to Tay,

'Let's have just one more of your lovely smiles, miss. That's great,' he enthused, clicking busily, and Tay smiled without effort this time, and had difficulty in controlling herself so that the smile did not turn into a laugh at Olive's expense.

She liked the reporters. They were a cheerfully informal crowd, casually friendly, with the exception of one who remained in the background, she noticed. He was a thin, weedy-looking man with a ferrety expression, who aimed his camera at them from a distance.

He homed in on Tay, however, when for a few minutes she found herself separated from Sven. The man held his camera at the ready, and there was an ingratiating smile on his face. 'What's it worth for an exclusive, miss?'

'I ...' Tay began, but before she could say any more Sven strode back to her side with swift steps, and the reporter scuttled away, and lost himself in the crowd of his colleagues.

Sven gave her a glacial look. 'Friend of yours?'

'No. I've never seen him before.'

'Strange.' His look was totally disbelieving. 'He's from the paper that leaked our photograph. But perhaps you contacted them by phone?'

'Don't start on that subject again!' Tay exploded. 'I told you, I had nothing to do with ...'

'Time for the route-briefing, ladies and gents. Can you

all get together now, please?' A marshal interrupted her angry denial, rounding up his flock for the route-briefing, and perforce Tay and Sven had to turn and follow his busy shepherding.

Olive was excluded from the briefing as well.

It was held in the ballroom of the hotel in which they were staying. An attractive buffet lunch had been laid on, at which all the competitors, with their back-up teams, could mingle and become acquainted.

Only a handful of women were present. The vast majority were men, all of them dedicated car enthusiasts, and many of them internationally famous in the rally field, an admixture that lured Olive like a bear attracted to honey.

'Only holders of blue cards are allowed into the route-briefing.' A polite but adamant official stopped Olive at the door, and ignoring her angry protests, he firmly barred her way, while waving Tay through into the room. 'Carry on in, miss,' he bade her. 'The photographers are waiting for you. They want a picture of all the lady competitors together, for one of the women's glossy magazines.'

The barely suppressed fury on Olive's face was not a pretty sight, and as Tay handed in her blue card to the official, and passed by into the room, the other girl hissed,

'You won't be smiling soon—you'll see!'

An hour of friendly relaxation passed before the presiding marshal called for their attention, and announced,

'Before we disperse, I'll just outline the essentials. You'll find the rest of your instructions in your route notes.'

Packs of printed pages were distributed amid a growing atmosphere of excited anticipation. There were to be five sections in all, one for each day of the Trials, which was to finish back at Nairobi on Friday, with a

final examination of the vehicles to discover how each
had stood up to its ordeal.

Back-up teams were to proceed along made-up roads
to given points along the route. This would take the
competing vehicles across country, through innumerable
hazards to be met along rough, unmade tracks, or no
tracks at all, relying on the skill of the crews at map-
reading, with only an occasional waymarker arrowing
the direction of a turn to help them on their way.

Competitors were to be started at short intervals, with
time-checks taken along the route to monitor their
performance on each section. The back-up teams, with
the less arduous task of travelling direct, on good roads,
would all start together after the last of the competing
cars was away.

Sven lined up with the other drivers to pull a number
out of a barrel, and drew the third starting place.

'That means we've got no time to lose,' he said, and
ushered his team briskly to the door. 'Let's go and collect
the campers right away.'

They hurried down the semi-circular flight of marble
steps fronting the hotel when an official came running
after them, waving a handful of papers.

'Mr Wallace,' he called to Ken, 'there's a paper short
in the packs. Here's your copy.'

'Oh, thanks very much.' Ken Wallace stopped and
took the paper, then turned back to hurry after Sven.

His haste was his undoing. As he turned, his foot
slipped on the smooth marble of the steps, and he
crashed the rest of the way down, landing in a crumpled
heap at the bottom.

'It's my arm,' he groaned, in white-faced dismay, as
Sven and Tay, and the Fielding mechanic, hurried to
pick him up. 'What a thing to happen now, of all times!'

'We'll take care of him, Mr Diamond. You carry on, or
you'll hold up the start.' The official who gave Ken the
paper hastened down the steps to join them. 'Don't
worry, we'll get him to hospital.'

'What'll you do, Mr Diamond?' Ken Wallace asked unhappily. 'You won't have a navigator now.'

'I'll manage on my own,' Sven replied, and Tay's ire rose.

'Oh, no, you won't,' she declared, as Ken was led away. 'I'm coming with you.'

'You?' Brilliant blue eyes glittered down at her, filled with a mixture of derision and scorn. 'You navigate for me?' Sven gave a short bark of a laugh. 'You'd never survive one day, let alone five, across country as wild as this. The Trials are an endurance test for the drivers and navigators, as well as for the vehicles.' His tone made his opinion of Tay's powers of endurance insultingly plain.

'You can't go on your own.' She controlled her rising fury with difficulty.

'Just watch me,' their owner taunted, and Tay's eyes flashed green fire.

'You know as well as I do that my father agreed to your using his engine in your vehicle on the understanding that a member of our own firm was part of the crew of the competing vehicle,' she argued. 'Now Ken's broken his arm, that leaves me in his place.'

She held the trump card, and Sven must know it.

'If you refuse to let me crew the vehicle with you, I'll cancel the entry for our engine,' she threatened. 'See if you can run your fabulous new camper without it!'

'You wouldn't dare,' he gritted.

'Try me!'

Defiantly, Tay steeled herself against his grim-visaged fury. The signed agreement between their two companies gave her the power to carry out her threat, and he knew it.

'A competing vehicle's no place for a woman.' Sven's expression was as unrelenting as his voice.

'You're as bad as Scott Fielding,' Tay declared. 'There are other women in the teams besides me.'

'They're not in the competing vehicles. They're in the back-up teams, the same as you are.'

'The same as I *was*,' she corrected him. 'I'm in the competing vehicle now.'

She had to trot to keep up with him. He accelerated his stride until even the lanky Fielding mechanic was hard pressed to match his pace, and as Tay panted breathlessly at his side, her anger flared to match his speed of walking.

'Don't imagine you can leave me behind,' she puffed angrily.

'We'll be away for four nights.'

'There are sleeping huts available. The marshal said so. And I can use Ken's sleeping bag.'

'You'll be the only woman among the competitors.'

'So what? There's safety in numbers.'

Sven cast her a baleful look. 'I'll see your father. He'll bring you to your senses.'

'Dad's in Mombasa for the day, following up an enquiry for some engines. It may surprise you, but Fieldings aren't the only firm who're interested in our products.'

'You've only got just over half an hour, sir,' the Fielding mechanic warned.

'Then I've got no time to argue with you,' Sven snapped at Tay, and with a set face he strode into the showrooms to collect the camper.

'There's nothing to argue about,' Tay retorted, and running ahead of him, she climbed into the passenger seat of the camper. Short of physically ejecting her from the seat, Sven could not leave her behind.

She watched him surreptitiously through the window, and saw him pause for an instant beside the other, smaller camper. He frowned down at his foot, and lightly toed the carpet.

'Pawing the ground,' Tay grinned to herself. 'Temper, temper!'

Then she had a moment's misgiving. Had she accidentally got into the wrong camper. The two were alike to look at. A panicky glance behind her brought reassurance. She was in the four-berth version, and seconds later, Sven swung into the cab beside her.

'If you insist on going through with this crazy escapade, you've only got yourself to blame for the consequences,' he growled.

'Get going, *partner*,' Tay returned, and with a glare that washed his hands of any responsibility towards her, Sven whipped the camper out of the showroom and on to the road, and soon they were lining up at the starting point in the car park of the hotel, with their number—three—prominently displayed at the front and rear of the vehicle.

'Be an angel and grab some things from my room for me, quickly, will you?' Tay begged one of the girls from the back-up teams urgently through the open cab window, as she strolled along to the starting line to see them off. 'Ken's had an accident, and I've taken his place, and I haven't got a stitch with me except what I'm wearing.'

She dared not get out of the cab to fetch anything for herself. If she did, Sven would almost certainly grab the opportunity to go without her, and she did not intend to give him the satisfaction of outwitting her.

Minutes later the girl ran back and thrust Tay's bulging shoulder bag into her hands through the camper window.

'I've put in everything for four nights in the bush. And good luck,' she grinned cheekily, and Tay's colour rose, as she felt Sven's eyes fixed on her.

To hide her confusion, she fiddled with the seat-harness straps, adjusting them from fitting Ken Wallace's much larger bulk to her own diminutive size, keeping her eyes lowered even when they were shortened to her satisfaction, so that she missed seeing the starter's flag sweep down.

The camper leapt forward like a live creature, taking her unawares, and jolting her back into her seat with a force that knocked the breath from her lungs.

'You might have warned me,' she protested, and without taking his eyes from off the road Sven snapped back,

'You're here to navigate, so keep your eyes open, and your wits about you. Watch out for the marker that arrows us off the road. It should be coming up ahead of us at any minute now.' Clearly he intended to make her work every inch of her passage.

Suddenly, Tay did not care. The sun shone from a gloriously blue sky. The speed was exhilarating, and in spite of Sven's open antagonism, her competitive spirit rose as the tyres whined over the smoothly surfaced road out of the city.

Her determination rose with it. She was not so tall or so physically strong as Ken Wallace, but she was equally good as a navigator.

'There's the marker.' She spied the black arrow on its white-painted wooden post, and pointed ahead of them with an eager finger. 'There, just in front of us.'

'It's a good job I saw it before you did, or we'd have overshot it by now,' growled Sven.

Tay scowled. 'I forgot you have to wait for ever for these campers to respond to the controls,' she shot back, chagrined that he had seen the marker first.

The next second her teeth came together with a snap that, if her tongue had been in the way, might have bitten it in two. With hardly any change of speed, Sven swung the camper at right angles off the road, and kangarooed it with a spine-shattering jolt into a decline feet deep, and yards in length, that was punctuated by boulders which threatened their very existence if the vehicle should bottom on any single one of them.

Tay wanted to shut her eyes as the vehicle clawed its way out of the hollow, the wheels sliding wildly on the loose surface. Instead, she forced them to remain open, and glared sideways at Sven. He grinned back.

'What's the matter?' He caught her glare, and his smile

widened. 'It was only a pothole. There'll be worse to come.'

Tay's temper rose in a rush. 'Where? I didn't notice any pothole,' she snapped back, and felt a glow of satisfaction at his startled look.

If anyone's nerve was going to crack, it would be Sven's, and not her own, she determined. She found that determination strained to the uttermost in the breathless hours that followed.

With pressed lips, she stifled a groan of sheer terror as the track tilted them into a dried-up watercourse, at a point on her map marked 'ford', but which, to her alarmed eyes, looked as deep as a ravine.

'The camper won't take it,' she gasped.

'No?' Sven answered laconically, and drove straight at the further bank.

Tay shut her eyes then. She could not help it. The camper tipped at a terrifying angle, pushing her back into her seat. She felt the vehicle buck and lurch and scrabble. And miraculously, start to climb.

She heard Sven laugh—an exulting challenge of a laugh, that defied the impossible odds. The laugh of a man determined to win, uncaring of the punishment he inflicted on the vehicle or himself. Or her.

The camper slid and juddered, and after what seemed to Tay a lifetime later, unbelievably it straightened out, and they were out of the watercourse, and bumping on again over more or less level ground.

She opened her eyes and stared her amazement, and Sven shouted at her impatiently, 'Keep your eyes on the map, for goodness' sake! There's a fork in the track ahead of us.'

'Go left,' Tay directed, with a hurried glance at her map, and wished he would slow down for a while.

'Can't you slow down for a minute or two, until I get my stomach back?' she shouted.

'And lose points? Not likely,' Sven retorted. 'If you

feel queasy, stick your head out of the window. I told you not to come.'

Which as good as told her that, now she was here, she must make the best of it, because she could expect no sympathy from him.

Temper acted as an instant restorative, and Tay forgot her ill-used organ as a glint of water showed ahead of them. An exciting mixture of animals wandered beside it.

'There's a zebra, and some gazelles.'

'Never mind the animals,' Sven shouted. 'Look for the marker arrow. We've got to turn somewhere near the water hole.'

'I can't see any marker.'

Desperately, Tay strained her eyes, questing the edge of the water, trying not to be distracted by the fascination of the variety of wild life assembled to drink. 'There it is!' she cried at last.

And then she gasped her dismay. 'I can't see which way the arrow's pointing—a zebra's standing in the way!'

In answer, Sven stood on the horn. The blast was ear-splitting, and it had the instant effect of setting the animals on the move.

Their going revealed the hidden arrow, and with a quick twist of the wheel Sven swung the camper into line and roared on, and within minutes a moving cloud of dust ahead of them betrayed the presence of another competitor.

'That's number two.' He identified the dust cloud. 'Shut the window and hold tight. I'm going to pass him.'

The driver of the vehicle in front must have seen them coming, although how anyone could see through such a dust-storm defeated Tay.

Realising that a rival was breathing down his neck, the driver of number two pulled out all the stops to squeeze the last ounce of speed from his vehicle.

Tay did not believe the vehicle was capable of going

any faster across such nightmarish terrain, but to her amazement the speedometer needle crept remorselessly upwards as Sven coaxed the protesting engine to even greater efforts.

Without the breeze from the windows to cool them, the heat inside the cab rapidly became intolerable, and perspiration added to her misery. She could not see through the windscreen.

'Slow down,' she burst out.

'Scared?' Sven jeered, and her expression tightened.

'Only for the camper,' she snapped, and subsided into simmering silence.

Sven's face was set. His eyes narrowed to pinpoints, to penetrate the blinding dust, every ounce of his concentration beamed upon his rival, so that it was doubtful if he would have heard her if she spoke again, anyway.

Inch by inch the two vehicles drew level, and there began a duel of nerves between the two drivers that made her hold her breath until she felt as if her lungs must burst.

The track narrowed, but still the other driver kept to the middle of it, forcing Sven to drive along its outer edge.

Something had to give way. It would probably be her spine, if Sven did not slow down soon.

It was the other car's engine that collapsed. It had been flogged beyond endurance, and suddenly the screaming mechanism died, in a cloud of hissing steam and smoke, and Sven and Tay were through.

To Tay's amazement, Sven drove straight on without stopping.

'We can't leave them here, out in the wilds like this, with a broken-down car!' she cried.

Sven shrugged. 'We're not here to act as a breakdown team.' He carried on driving.

It was callous, inhuman. And there was absolutely nothing she could do about it. She strained her eyes anxiously towards the rear.

'Relax, they're O.K.' Sven glanced in his rear view mirror. 'They're not hurt. They're getting out of the car. We'll warn the marshals there's a breakdown when we get to the check-point at Nakuru. The back-up teams should have reached there by now.'

'We'll need the back-up team ourselves, if we keep going at this pace,' Tay prophesied. 'I could do with some spare vertebrae myself.'

'Sorry you came?' Sven taunted.

'I wouldn't have missed it for the world,' she snapped, incensed by his 'I told you so' grin.

If he hoped she would opt out now, and transfer to the back-up vehicle when they reached Nakuru, he was to be disappointed although it cost her every ounce of willpower to steel her mind against the temptation.

She ached all over. She felt as if every inch of her body had been pummelled into black and blue bruises. She had been shouted at and frightened almost out of her wits. And she was caked in grit and perspiration from head to toe.

And there were still four more days—and nights—to come.

CHAPTER FOUR

NAKURU had an air of carnival about it when they arrived in the outskirts a short time later. Crowds of enthusiastic spectators lined the streets, to watch the competing vehicles come in, and their wide smiles matched the bright colours of their clothes, to lend a cheerful welcome to the weary crews.

After the excruciating tracks they had just endured, it was bliss to ride over smooth road surfaces again, and Tay's spirits rose as she waved back to the crowds. They called out friendly greetings when Sven slammed the camper to a halt at the check-point, and leapt down from the driving seat to get their card time-stamped by the presiding marshal.

That done, Sven pushed his way back through the people crowded round the camper, allowing his hand to be caught and shaken umpteen times on the way. He opened the door on Tay's side, and bade her,

'Come on down. We've got half an hour's rest period here, for something to eat and drink.'

Tay doubted if she was capable of moving. Summoning up her last remaining reserves of energy, she undid her seat-harness and winced as she gingerly eased herself round, preparatory to descending.

'Feeling stiff?' taunted Sven. 'That's nothing to what you'll be by tomorrow morning.'

Before she realised what he was about to do, he reached up both arms and plucked her from the seat, and set her down beside him on the ground, keeping an arm round her waist in order to steady her.

'I can manage,' she claimed, in a tone as stiff as her aching limbs.

'Sure you can,' Sven mocked. He watched her stumbling walk. 'I just didn't want to lose you in the crowd, that's all. Come and have a snack while you've got the chance.'

Which boded ill for the timing of their next meal, and made Tay follow his advice with alacrity as an official doled out sandwiches and cold drinks. The sharp fruit juice was nectar to her dehydrated throat, and she gulped it down thirstily.

'Where's our other camper?' Sven enquired of the official with a frown, his eyes searching the line of back-up vehicles parked behind the check-point.

'Its engine passed out at the starting-point, Mr Diamond.' One of the mechanics strolled across to join them. 'The last I saw of it, it was being towed back to your agents' workshops.'

'We'll service you, if you like, Sven,' another man offered generously. 'There's enough petrol and water here to fuel Concorde.'

'Thanks, lads, I won't forget what you've done,' Sven accepted, as the two mechanics from the opposing teams set about topping up the travel-stained camper.

'So much for the famous Hilliard engine,' Sven remarked, as Tay climbed stiffly back into the cab beside him, when the rest period was over. 'It didn't even get past the starting-post.'

'If you think so little of our engine, why are you so keen to merge with our company?' she flashed back.

'Put it down to compassion,' he drawled. 'You need us more than we need you, Copper.'

'Compassion? You?' she cried. 'There'll never be a time when I need you!'

She meant 'we', not 'I', but she was too incensed to correct the personalisation. Sven's arched eyebrows told her he had noticed it, and hurriedly she sidetracked.

'The breakdown must be due to your mechanic's atrocious driving.'

What other answer could there be? she wondered worriedly.

Ken Wallace had burned midnight oil for weeks to bring both the engines to a pitch of perfection, and he had personally supervised their fitting into the campers, and himself tested the results, and pronounced that he was satisfied.

Why could her father not have remained in Nairobi for the start of the Trials, instead of having to travel to Mombasa to follow up an enquiry for their engines? After such an ignominious start, would the enquirer still be interested?

Tay's mind churned with unanswered questions, but she schooled her face to hide her concern as Sven said with sublime confidence,

'It can't be our driver's fault. All our men are trained to Fielding standards.'

As if that answered everything, she fumed, and set herself to dent his arrogance.

'If Fielding standards are the same as yours, that explains why the engine's passed out,' she claimed. 'You called me a lunatic.' How his insult rankled still! 'But my driving's nothing compared to the performance you gave this afternoon!'

He more than exceeded it during the hours that followed, in the last, gruelling stretch of the day that ended not a moment too soon for Tay at the night-stop sited in the bush.

She crawled out of the cab, too exhausted to appreciate the small, thatch-topped huts, like a mini Olympic village, that had been specially erected to accomodate the contestants. Her whole body throbbed with weariness, and all she wanted to do was to stretch Ken's sleeping-bag on the nearest flat surface and creep into its comforting folds and oblivion.

The crew of number one car were already unloading their gear, and dazedly she registered their surprise at her

appearance among them, but explanations about Ken's
accident were beyond her for the moment.

Her nostrils caught the smell of hot food from the
nearest hut, but it failed to tempt her. Whatever the
marshals had prepared for the crews would have to wait
until she was rested. She was too exhausted to eat now.

'You'll find the food in the cool-box under the left-
hand bunk.' He looked up from where he was crouched,
examining one of the rear tyres. 'You cook the supper,
while I check the camper for damage. The portable
stove's next to the cool-box.'

'C-cook *supper*?' She felt as if her ears must be
deceiving her. She had not got the strength to eat, let
alone start on domestic chores.

'That's what I said. Food's provided for us at the rest-
stops during the day, but we have to cater for ourselves at
night. Read the rules.' Sven scowled impatiently when
she made no move to get the equipment. 'There it is, right
in front of you.' He reached in a long arm to the back of
the camper and began to pull out an assortment of items,
which he piled into Tay's limp arms.

'Cooker, saucepan, can of beans, can of sardines—
have whichever you like,' he invited. 'Here's the bread.'
He wedged a long French roll under Tay's chin, and
added, 'Here's some tinned fruit for afters. I presume
you're capable of warming up a can of beans?' he asked,
as she stared at him in stunned silence.

His sarcasm stung life back into her flagging frame.

'Provided you haven't forgotten the tin opener,' she bit
back, and wished wearily that he had. It would provide
her with the perfect excuse to leave him with the loaf of
dry bread for his supper, which was all he deserved.

The ghost of a smile showed on Sven's face, and he
rummaged again, and came up with a tin opener, cutlery,
and a couple of enamel plates.

'Use the hut next to number one's crew,' he told her,

and without more ado he ducked under the camper again and began to examine the axle.

Tay felt a wrathful urge to use his recumbent legs as a football, but reflecting that he would probably be capable of kicking her back if she did, she resisted the temptation. Her abused body was sore enough already, without risking further punishment.

Under any other circumstances, the doll's house proportions of the hut would have enchanted Tay, but the darkness inside it was complete, and in desperation she switched on the spare inspection lamp to enable her to see what she was doing.

The light did not help her much. The stove seemed determined to become her personal Waterloo. Try as she might, she could not coax it to remain alight for more than a few minutes at a time.

'Drat the beastly thing!' she muttered furiously as, for the umpteenth time, the stove began to show signs of life, only to expire again the moment she turned away from it to open the can of beans.

'It's easy to see you haven't used one of these before.' A dark, bearded face laughed down into her own, and the young giant who drove the first car removed the stove from her willing hands and manhandled it expertly into glowing life. 'Don't take it too close to the hut,' he cautioned her, 'in case you have a spill, and it sets fire to the thatch.'

Tay's stammered thanks followed him back to his own meal, and she hurriedly beheaded two cans of beans which she poured into the saucepan. As she did so, something small and persistent tickled the back of her neck, and she slapped at it shudderingly.

'Ugh, mosquitoes!'

They whined round her like fighter planes. Tay slapped and flapped with one hand, while with the other she desperately tried to stir the contents of the saucepan to prevent them from burning.

A small, hard, wriggling body banged straight into her face, and dropped down the opened neck of her shirt. Tay abandoned the beans to their fate, and shrieked unashamedly,

'Sven!'

'Switch off the light—it's attracting the bugs. You'll have them blundering into the cooking if you're not careful.'

Not one word of concern that a bug had blundered into her bra!

Sven loomed over her, but not to help her rid herself of the invader. He leaned down. There was a sharp click, and the light went out.

'How can I see?' Tay began, frantically shaking herself to get rid of the insect.

'You don't have to see, to cook beans,' he growled. 'Just keep the lid on the saucepan, so the bugs don't fall into it and get cooked along with the supper. Have you cut the bread?'

'I haven't had time,' Tay snapped. She sounded like a harassed housewife, she thought crossly, and hated Sven for the undisguised amusement on his face.

'I'll do it,' he offered. 'Hold out your plate.'

He dismembered the French roll with three decisive slashes of the knife, poured beans on to the plates in equal shares, and said with satisfaction as he started to eat, 'I'm ready for this.'

No word of praise, let alone thanks, for cooking his supper for him. Tay glowered at her own plateful, and the beans stared blandly back, innocent of bugs, and suddenly she realised that she, too, was ravenously hungry.

It was surprising what such a simple meal could accomplish. The food rejuvenated her to an extent that she even volunteered to make the coffee, telling Sven firmly, 'I'll do it. You've done the driving.'

She felt astonished at herself for wanting to do

anything at all to help him, when he was going out of his way deliberately to drive her to the limits of her endurance, hoping that his cruelty would make her opt out of the Trials and rid him of her unwanted company.

'You roll your sleeping-bag on the platform at the back of the hut,' he bade her when, the meal finished, and the implements washed and stowed back in the camper, her eyelids began to droop, and she could hide her weariness no longer. 'I'll sleep by the hut door.'

It dawned upon her for the first time that the huts were built to accommodate two. She felt her cheeks grow hot in the darkness, with a fiery mixture of indignation and confusion. In spite of her brave assertion to Sven at the beginning of the Trials, now it came to the crunch she did not feel brave at all.

She could feel Sven's eyes watching her. Reading her uncertainty, and secretly laughing at it? It was too dark to see his expression properly, which meant it was too dark for him to see hers, she realised thankfully, and slapped viciously at a mosquito.

The insect gave her an idea, and a ready-made excuse at the same time.

'I'm not going to sleep under that thatch with all these creepy-crawlies wandering about,' she declared with a shiver that was not altogether feigned. 'I'm going to sleep in the camper.'

Pleased with her strategy, she rose. Sven shrugged. 'Please yourself. I thought you might enjoy the novelty of sleeping in a hut, that's all.'

'The camper will be just as much a novelty for me. I'll let you know how it measures up, in the morning,' she promised with barbed sweetness, and bidding him good night, she escaped to the vehicle, and shut the door firmly behind her before he had a chance to reply.

She found Ken's sleeping-bag tossed on the one bunk, proving that he had the same idea, and it took only minutes for Tay to undress and zip herself into its folds, and with a sigh of pure relief, she sank back and allowed her weary body to relax.

A sound caught her ears—the faint but unmistakable turning of the door handle.

Tay sat abruptly upright in the bunk, clutching the sleeping-bag round her. The camper door opened wide, and a dark figure stood outlined against the night.

'Who's there?' she called out sharply.

'It's me.' said Sven, and stepping into the camper, he shut the door behind him.

'You can't come in here.' Tay stammered. 'You ... you're sleeping in the hut.'

'I *was* sleeping in the hut.' His tone was even. 'Now I'm sleeping in the camper.'

'B-but ...' She stared up at him, appalled.

He had not abandoned his campaign to make her change her mind about the merger, after all. With dreadful clarity, Scott Fielding's words came back to mock her.

'Compromise her, if you like.'

And by her own insistence on coming with Sven, she had made it dreadfully easy for him to do just that.

Tay swallowed on a throat gone suddenly dry. 'I—I've changed my mind,' she blurted out. 'I think I'll sleep in the hut, after all.'

'Make up your mind.' Sven's voice was harsh. 'I'm too tired to go cantering about from the hut to the camper, and back again, just to please you. We either sleep here, or in the hut.'

We ...

He meant it. Tay stared up at him, her eyes wide pools of consternation in the darkness. 'You ... I ...' She ground to a halt.

'If you imagine you're going to occupy either the camper or the hut on your own, you can think again,' he disabused her. 'There's a crowd of young bloods out there in the huts who might have other sports in mind besides motor trials.'

'They wouldn't.' Tay recovered her voice.

'While I'm responsible for you, I'm not risking it,' he retorted, and added with an unexpected laugh in his voice that came clearly to her through the darkness, 'now, if you want to preserve your maidenly modesty, close your eyes and turn over until I'm in my own sleeping-bag.'

He loomed over her, unnervingly large in the close confines of the camper, and Tay sat rigidly, her arms hugging her knees, her frozen mind wrestling with the implications of what he said.

He was not responsible for her. She was responsible for herself. She opened her mouth to tell him so when he bent down, and reached into the bunk.

In the confined space there was nowhere for her to get away from him. The next moment, his arms went under her, and she found herself lying down, and her sleeping-bag zipped up to her chin with impatient fingers. And then Sven's arms were hard round her again, rolling her swiftly over on her side to face the window.

'Close your eyes and go to sleep,' he told her in a rough-sounding voice, and turning his back on her, he began to strip his shirt over his head.

Hurriedly Tay closed her eyes, but she could not go to sleep. Her strained senses remained agonisingly aware of every slight movement Sven made. The aisle was so narrow betweeen the two bunks that she could feel the pressure of him leaning against her own as he bent down to undo his shoes.

She forced herself to lie still until the pressure eased, and then the opposite bunk creaked, and she heard the sound of a zip being drawn along as Sven slid into his sleeping-bag, and minutes later, his even breathing told her he slept.

She could open her eyes now. But her heavy lids

refused the task, and she lay on her side where Sven had
rolled her, and drifted into oblivion, feeling irrationally
secure because he was sleeping in the opposite bunk.

At first, she could not identify the sound that wakened
her.

Lightning from a faraway electric storm flickered
across the sky. Tay listened for the sound of thunder, but
none came, so it could not have been that.

And then she heard it—a low, soft, crunching noise,
indescribably dreadful. It made her flesh creep to listen
to it.

She strained her ears, and it came again, louder this
time. Nearer. It sounded as if it was coming from almost
underneath the camper.

Another flicker of lightning, and a coughing roar
shook the night, coming from somewhere close to hand.
At the sound, a low, crouching creature slunk under the
camper window, and another. A third appeared, and
Tay's overstretched nerves snapped.

'Sven! Sven, wake up!'

Frantically she reached across the narrow aisle,
grabbed the sleeping-bag on the opposite bunk with both
hands, and shook its contents into startled life.

'What the . . .?'

'Sven, get up! There's something eating . . . *something*,' she gulped, 'out there!'

The awful roaring went on and on. The night air
reverberated with the noise, and with a shaking finger
Tay pointed out of the window to yet more slinking forms
round the camper.

'Hyena,' Sven identified them at a glance. 'I'll have a
look to see what they're up to.'

'Don't go outside.' she implored, and grabbed at his
arm in order to keep him with her. 'They might . . . they
might . . .' she ground to a halt.

'Would it matter very much to you if they did,
Copper?' he asked her, and she stared at him, straining

her eyes to pierce the darkness, that made it impossible to read the expression on his face.

'I . . . I . . .' He was goading her. 'I don't know the way back to Nairobi by myself,' she said stiffly, and wondered if that was the only reason it might trouble her.

She was conscious of his closeness as he leaned down across her bunk, his deep chest pressing against her as he bent to peer out of the window on her side, probing the mysteries of the night.

Without warning, Sven chuckled, and Tay jumped violently.

'Hey, you're trembling all over,' he discovered.

He extricated himself from the bunk, and sat on the edge of it, and scooped her, sleeping bag and all, into the shelter of his arms.

'I heard something feeding . . . out there.' She shuddered again at the awful memory.

'The hyenas have managed to prise the lid off the scrap bin.' Sven smiled, and his teeth gleamed whitely in the gloom. 'They're having a high old time on the left-overs from the hut suppers.'

'Is that all?' Tay stared doubtfully up at him. 'I thought . . .'

'The lions have got enough choice of supper out there,' Sven assured her amusedly. 'They don't need to come hunting for Trials crews. Though they might regard you as a tasty morsel,' he teased, and feeling her stiffen, he tightened his arms comfortingly round her.

'Don't worry,' he assured her. 'We're safe here, so long as no one is silly enough to wander about on their own in the darkness. The marshals warned everyone clearly enough of the danger, if they do.'

Nothing had warned Tay of the dangers she faced from within herself.

Sven folded her to him, turning her face against his bare shoulders, and stroking her soft curls with a gentle, soothing motion that sent shivers of quite another sort coursing through her. He bent his head, and his mouth followed the direction of his hand. And then his fingers stopped stroking and cupped her chin instead, and his lips brought the lightning from the sky to burn her throat and cheeks.

The delicate blue veins of her temples throbbed wildly to their touch, and she wondered if he could feel their swift, uneven beat, only to forget her wonder as his mouth captured hers, and blotted out the sounds of the night outside with a deep, searching pressure that went on and on.

The lion stopped roaring, and the whole earth seemed to hold its breath. The silence in the camper was complete. And then, slowly, lingeringly, his lips brushing across her mouth in a long, tantalising caress, Sven let her go.

Tay lay in his arms, too dazed to speak. Beyond the camper windows lay a wild and primitive world, where creatures stalked the night, hunting their prey. And inside the camper—inside herself—she was shocked to discover feelings that were equally wild, and just as primitive, as anything the bushland might harbour. Fierce longings that were strange, and wholly frightening, and that she did not have the first idea how she could begin to handle.

They added to her violent trembling, and terrified lest Sven should guess the effect he was having on her, she blamed it on the lions.

'I wish they'd stop that awful roaring. I'll never get back to sleep while they're making that noise.'

'At least it tells you where they are,' Sven said philosophically. 'Those that hunt in silence are the ones to fear.'

Like Sven.

What would he say if she told him she knew of Scott's despicable plan, she wondered. She stirred uneasily, pulling away from him. 'I'm all right now. I . . . I'm sorry I disturbed you.'

'Stay awake, and talk for a while.' He firmed his arms round her, resisting her move away from him. 'If you give yourself time to calm down, you'll settle off to sleep all the quicker in the long run.'

How did he imagine she could calm down, while she still rested in his arms? Tay wondered raggedly. Aloud, she said,

'What do you want to talk about?'

'You,' he said. She could feel him smile down at her in the darkness. 'You've got an unusual name, for instance. How did you come by it?'

He was talking to calm her, as he would calm a frightened child. But her feelings were the reverse of childish, and she resented his patronage.

'I was named after the Scottish river,' she told him shortly.

She did not want to talk about herself. With the same instinct for self-preservation that protected the wild creatures in the game reserve outside, she steeled herself to resist any encroachment by Sven that would leave her more vulnerable to his wiles.

Adroitly, she redirected the conversation to less dangerous channels.

'Your own name isn't all that common for an Englishman.' She gave him a lead, and let out a pent-up breath of relief when he followed it.

'It's my godfather's name. He's Sven Jorgssen, the film producer. He's a friend of my family.'

'Are they in the film business, too?' Tay asked, interested in spite of herself.

'No, they're in shipping—the Diamond Line. My father happens to be the current Chairman.'

'The Diamond Line?' echoed Tay, unable to conceal her surprise. 'Then what brings you working for Fieldings?'

The Diamond Line was one of the oldest shipping companies in the business, and easily the richest and most successful. Moreover, it was still owned exclusively by the one family.

'Easy,' he answered, and she felt his shrug. 'I wanted to test my own abilities in the cut and thrust of the market place, before I joined the family firm.'

'I suppose it isn't a bad policy,' she admitted. 'At least that way, you get a varied experience in other companies besides your own.'

'It's a policy that's paid off over the years,' Sven agreed. 'My two older brothers each did the same thing. It allows us to find our own level in the outside world, and by the time we're ready to join the family firm, we've discovered our own strengths and weaknesses, and gained a broad base of experience between us, that helps to keep the Line abreast of our competitors.'

Tay privately doubted if this particular scion of the Diamond family had discovered any weakness. She asked curiously,

'Are you the youngest in the family?'

The unexpected insight into Sven's background intrigued her. For a man whose assured wealth meant he was not obliged to work, his reputation for doing just that, and succeeding at it superlatively well, said a lot for his strength of character.

'Not quite. I've got a younger sister. There are five of us altogether, three boys, and two girls. Both of my parents are still alive.'

The softness of his voice as he spoke of his family told Tay more than words how close they were to one another, and she felt an unexpected prick of envy for those people who were capable of producing that gentle tone from him.

'I'm the only one,' she said, and there was an unconscious wistfulness in her voice as she spoke. 'Mother died when I was still quite small.'

'No boy-friends?' Sven's lips stroked disarming sympathy across her forehead, and she pulled away from his touch, alarmed by the smouldering fires it fanned into life inside her.

'No one serious,' she said stiffly, and could have kicked herself, for falling into such an obvious trap. She should have invented a fiancé of rugger-player proportions, preferably a karate expert for good measure.

It was like Sven's cheek to probe into her personal affairs, she thought resentfully.

He had taken swift advantage of her earlier fright when she was at her most vulnerable, and beguiled her by his false gentleness into allowing her guard to slip. The instant it did, he was through, and breaching the defences she had so carefully erected against him. He did not miss a trick. But she was over her panic now, and ready to fight back.

'What about you? Have you got a girl-friend waiting in the wings?'

Tay turned the subject away from herself, and back to Sven.

'No one serious.' He mocked her with her own words. 'There's plenty of time, after I join the family firm, and can lead a more settled existence than I'm doing now.'

Which hinted that he regarded his directorship at Fieldings as a short-term commitment. It did not prevent him from exerting himself to unscrupulous lengths on their behalf, Tay condemned him silently.

What kind of woman would Sven eventually marry? she wondered. He was rich, handsome, and successful—a deb's dream, in fact. Would he marry someone as hard and ambitious as he was himself? Someone who would act the perfect hostess at his dinner parties, and glory in the glamour and social standing that being the wife of a shipping magnate would bring in its train?

Someone like Olive?

The thought was oddly at variance with the affectionate way he had spoken of his present family. Tay tilted her head back to look up into his face, struck by the contrast between the Sven she knew and the man she sensed he might be among his own kin.

She shook her thoughts away from the traitorous thought, and realised with a start that Sven's face was reaching down close, and closer, to her own.

'In the meantime,' he murmured, carrying on the thread of his conversation, 'in the meantime, there's no reason why I shouldn't have fun.' His lips stroked along the arched curve of her throat, seeking the tender base.

Have fun. That was what Olive had told Tay to do. Was this what she had hinted at?

With a convulsive jerk, Tay wrenched herself out of his arms. 'Find someone else to have your fun with!' she spat. 'I'm not a candidate.'

She longed to strike out at the white, mocking grin that split his well cut lips. But her arms were still trappped inside her sleeping bag. With a quick wriggle she shuffled to the other side of the bunk, away from him, and flattened herself against the window, as far away from him as she could get, and stared back at him with blazing eyes.

'It's a bit late for you to act the prude,' growled Sven. 'You insisted on coming in Ken's place, even though you knew all the rest of the competitors would be men. I tried to make you stay behind.'

'I came to compete in the Trials,' she flashed, 'not to provide you with what you call fun. So far as I'm concerned, you're not the prize.'

'I never reckoned to be,' he drawled, adding insultingly, 'never fear, Copper. You're quite safe with me.'

Swiftly, he leaned back across the bunk and pulled her towards him, and his lips searched, and found, hers, pressing them back against her parted teeth with a swift, hard, bruising kiss that was an insult in itself.

''Night, Copper,' he mocked. 'Sweet dreams.'

And slipping into his own bunk, he rolled over and presented his back to Tay, and was swiftly asleep, leaving her wide-eyed in the darkness to wrestle with the turmoil of her thoughts.

Sven would be a prize most girls would dream of. But if she could not control the violent upsurge of emotion which he managed to arouse in her with such humiliating ease whenever he touched her, she realised with swiftly racing pulse, he might become her own personal nightmare.

CHAPTER FIVE

'GET up, Tay. It's time to cook breakfast. It'll be light in an hour, and we're second away this morning.'

Hard hands shook her cruelly awake. Hard words dragged her mercilessly out of the blissful cocoon of sleep, and back into an agonised world where every bone in her body seemed about to part company with its fellow, and screamed its own personal anguish at the torment of separation.

Tay never knew she had so many places in her body that were capable of feeling such excruciating pain. She felt stiff and sore from head to toe. She groaned feebly, and closed her eyes against the unwanted world.

'It's no good lying there moaning. Get up and cook breakfast, while I fill up the camper. *Get up*, I said,' Sven insisted.

He did not wait for her to obey him. She had no intention of doing so. 'Cook your own . . .' she began rebelliously.

Before she could finish her sentence, he reached into the bunk and grabbed her, and pulled her bodily on to her feet. With angry hands he ripped open the zip of her sleeping-bag, and with nothing to keep it up, it dropped limply on to the floor about her feet.

The shock of his action brought Tay fully awake.

'You . . .' she blazed furiously, and her hands flew up to cover her exposed shoulders.

'Save the insults until you've cooked my breakfast.'

Sven's gaze raked over her, taking in her flaming face, her brief cotton nightie, her bare feet. His eyes were hard, unmerciful, and uninterested.

'I'll give you exactly five minutes to get dressed. If

you're not finished by the time I come back, I'll button you into your gear myself!' He turned his back on her , and strode purposefully outside.

Tay's shoe hit the camper door just as he closed it behind him. She ground her teeth as his mocking laugh floated back to her, and then had to grit them hard to prevent another anguished groan from escaping her lips, as the movement of throwing her shoe at Sven caused spasms of pain to shoot through her stiffened limbs.

She left her shoes unlaced. The effort of bending down to tie them up hurt too much, and they slopped up and down on her feet as, five minutes later, she tottered down the camper steps, clutching the portable stove, and a supply of tinned sausages and bread in her arms.

Sven's grin, as he surveyed her from the bottom of the steps, acted like sandpaper on her sore frame and even more sorely tried temper.

'*Don't*, unless you want a burnt offering for your breakfast,' she warned him.

'I wasn't going to say a word,' he assured her, his maddening grin growing even wider. 'I was going to tie up your shoelaces for you, before you trip over them and come a cropper. I'd hate you to drop the stove. It's the only one we've got, and it's precious.'

She glowered at him as he pressed her creakily down on to the camper steps, and went on one knee himself in front of her, bending with an enviable ease that betrayed no sign of her own painfulness.

With swift fingers, he knotted and bowed the shoelace, then looked up into her face and said, 'You're safe now.'

How safe?

His eyes danced with merriment at her expense, laughing into hers from a vivid blue well of carefree fun, and Tay's heart did an odd backwards flip inside her breast. It had executed the same disconcerting manoeuvre the night before when he kissed her, and the repetition was all the warning she needed.

'Arise, sir knight,' she snapped sarcastically, and to her chagrin found that she herself could not.

Her arms were encumbered by food and cooking utensils, and her stiff legs had not got the necessary push of themselves to raise her unaided from the steps.

Sven settled her dilemma. He reached down, and pulled her, stove, breakfast supplies and all, on to her feet. 'I'll give you a rub down, if you like,' he taunted her stiffness. 'There's some grease in the camper.'

The offer was enough to speed Tay on her way. The mere thought of Sven's hands smoothing over her aching limbs gave her goose-pimples all over. Hurriedly, she refused. 'No, thanks. It's probably axle-grease, anyway.' And with her nose in the air she forced her legs to walk as near normally as their protesting muscles would allow, and took her burden to the hut.

The air was chilled with a thick, early-morning mist, which was an added incentive to get the stove going. Doubting her own ability in that direction, Tay looked round hopefully for her bearded helpmate of the night before, but the other crews were all busy on their own account, preparing for the day ahead, and no one volunteered more than a brief 'good morning'.

She would have to tackle the mechanical monster herself. Carefully, she kept her back turned towards Sven, so that he should not see her and jeer at her inexpertise, and tackled her *bête noire* with grim determination.

The effort hurt, but the glow of satisfaction when the stove fired, and kept going, more than compensated for the pain, and triumphantly she emptied sausages into the pan, and started to slice the loaf. She was halfway through cutting the second chunk of bread when she heard the engine of the camper start up.

She spun round, grimacing at the protest her stiff muscles made at the sudden movement. Sven was at the wheel of the camper, and it was already beginning to roll.

Forgetting the breakfast, Tay scrambled to her feet and started to run towards it.

'Sven! Sven!'

He must have heard her, but he did not look round. The camper gathered speed and disappeared into the mist, and Tay stumbled to a disbelieving halt.

'Sven?' she croaked.

He had deserted her. Started off, and left her behind, just as she had been afraid he would do. Cunningly, he had bided his time until her back was turned, and she was engrossed in cooking the breakfast, and he had grabbed his opportunity and gone.

An upsurge of anger and panic, and some other emotion that she could not define, but which was stronger than either of the other two, rooted her, shaking, to the dusty ground.

Sven had left her flat.

The marshals would rescue her—he knew that. Physically, she was quite safe. Mentally, she felt as if she were about to erupt. She would be the laughing stock of the entire Trials when it became known that Sven had abandoned her. *And he did not care.* She hated him with a fierceness that frightened her.

'Your breakfast's burning, miss.'

What was breakfast? What was anything, compared to the enormity of what Sven had just done to her?

Suddenly Tay wanted to cry.

'Miss, your breakfast's ...'

She did not wait to hear any more. Before the tears overflowed and shamed her irretrievably in front of the other crews, she turned and fled for the blessed shelter of the hut.

'Heaven help the man you marry!' Sven's voice reached her from the region of the stove. 'You can't even cook tinned sausages without burning them to a cinder!'

A clatter of enamel plates and an impatient scraping sound punctuated his scorn, and Tay dashed a hand

across her wet cheeks and peered incredulously through
the hut doorway.

Sven glared across at her from the stove. 'It's a good
job I rescued these when I did. Another minute, and
they'd have been uneatable.'

'You ... you took the camper away,' she accused.

She surveyed his large reassuring bulk and that of the
camper, parked back in its place beside the hut where it
had spent the night. Had she fallen asleep from sheer
weariness, and dreamed it all? Turned her fears into a
daytime nightmare?

'I went to fill up the petrol tank. I told you I was going
to.' Sven gave her a penetrating look. 'Come and eat your
breakfast,' he commanded. 'We're due at the starting-
line in half an hour.'

Scorched sausages were ambrosia.

Sven ate with a concentrated attention, and spoke in
monosyllables. He made no reference to the previous
night by either word or look. He had probably forgotten
all about it, his mind on the challenge of the day ahead.

'I see you've rescued your breakfast,' the bearded
young giant from number one car laughed as he passed
by.

'All except one sausage,' Tay felt recovered enough to
laugh back.

'Leave that for the hyenas. Did you hear them having a
rummage in the garbage bins last night?'

'I heard them.' In spite of the sunshine, she shivered at
the memory. 'And the lions.'

'Oh, lions only roar *after* they've eaten.' the bearded
one answered with conviction, and passed on.

Tay cast Sven a suspicious look. Did he know that?
And had he played on her fears to make her more
receptive to his kisses? The hard knot began to form
again inside her, tightening uncomfortably round her
breakfast.

The usual crowd of locals gathered to see them off.

Children with melting dark eyes, and bright, laughing faces ran in and out among the competitors, excited by this sudden influx of people into their quiet community.

'It's market day somewhere,' Sven remarked ruefully, as he was obliged to slow the camper to a crawl to negotiate knots of people, the occasional bicycle, a country bus, and now and then a weighted-down lorry, carrying produce and people in such abundance that it overflowed across the sides, leaving the lorry itself barely visible.

More and more appeared as if by magic, the further they travelled along the dusty road. The pedestrians all paused in their journey to wave, as the Trials cars went by, the heavy loads which the women carried with such apparent ease upon their heads, atop their bright kerchiefs, seeming to make not a whit of difference to their cheerful smiles.

'Try it yourself,' Sven suggested when Tay expressed her admiration of them for the umpteenth time.

'I should probably end up with a slipped disc, or drop my load,' she prophesied, and waved back, and wished there were time to stop and walk along with them and make friends.

But speed was a whiplash, driving them on, and soon they left the villages behind, and were out again into wild country, climbing sharply up inclines that brought the camper bonnet almost back on to their own noses.

'You need a helicopter on this kind of country,' she gasped, and marvelled at the surety of Sven's judgement as he swung the camper into each worsening bend, turning it at angles she would not have thought the vehicle capable of, while calculating to a nicety exactly how much slide the wheels would take, to give them a margin of safety at the very edge.

They reached the top, and cool, sweet air blew through the camper windows, laving their arms and faces like a benediction after the heat of the previous day, and the

whole breathtaking panorama of the Rift Valley lay like
a living map below them.

There was no time to appreciate the view. Other
competitors snarled at their heels. The car in front must
be overtaken, if humanly possible. Without pause, Sven
plunged the camper down again, through dark lines of
conifers. Down still further, among the leafy greenery,
back on to the scorching heat of a wide, flat plain, with
acacia trees, and, Tay saw longingly, giraffe feeding from
their thorny branches.

This was a country to linger in, not to hurry through.
But hurry they must, or lose points, and although her
heart grieved at the waste, her mind acknowledged the
necessity, and she dragged her eyes away from the
giraffes, and fixed them determinedly on the map she
hugged on her knees.

'There should be a fork in the track just ahead. Go
right,' she directed Sven.

To vindicate her map-reading, the fork duly appeared,
and so did a lorry, loaded past the cab roof with logs, and
boasting a driver who either did not see them, or did not
care, or both.

With suicidal carelessness, he changed his mind
suddenly at the fork, and from travelling left, he swung to
the right with a suddenness that wrung a muffled
ejaculation from Sven. There was no time to brake. The
lorry swung across their bows within inches of their front
bumper.

'Hold tight!' Sven yelled.

He wrenched the wheel hard over. The camper keeled
at an angle that made light of the way Tay had bent it
over on the test-track at home. She hunched into her seat-
harness, and braced herself for the crash. And then
miraculously, Sven righted it. The lorry blundered on,
unscathed, and Tay let out a gusty breath of relief, just as
the offside front wheel clipped a pile of jagged rock, and
the front tyre exploded with a bang like a bomb.

Sven slewed the vehicle to a halt and flung open the door. 'Jump out, quickly!' he shouted at Tay. 'Unstrap the spare wheel from inside the camper, while I jack it up at the front.'

He ran round to open the back of the vehicle to get the tools, almost before Tay had time to unstrap herself from her seat-harness.

This, then, was the reason he had loaded their vehicle with so many spares, as well as the back-up camper. She reached the spare wheel as Sven vanished round towards the front of the vehicle, with the jack in his hands. The strap that held the spare wheel was stiff, and the buckle was tight, and it took all of her wiry strength to get it to budge.

'Stop jacking for a minute, can't you?' she shouted irritably. 'How do you expect me to stand up while you're tilting the floor at this angle?'

'There isn't time to stop,' Sven shouted back. 'Hurry up, will you?' He carried on jacking.

'I can't hurry while . . . oh!' gasped Tay. The buckle gave way suddenly, and the sharp camber of the vehicle raised on the jack did the rest.

The wheel tilted away fron the wall, and leaned on her. She exerted all her wiry strength to try to withstand its weight, but it was too heavy for her light frame. Her feet skidded under her on the sloping floor, and she landed in a heap against the far wall, with the wheel on top of her, pinning her down.

'Help!' she shouted.

Sven rounded the back of the camper at a run. 'Can't you even unbuckle a wheel without getting yourself into trouble?' He lifted them both simultaneously. 'Are you hurt?'

'No, I couldn't get up, that's all,' Tay glared. 'It was your fault! If you'd stopped jacking for a second or two, when I asked you . . .'

'We haven't got a second or two to spare,' Sven

responded brusquely. 'Come and help me to put the bolts on.' He rolled the wheel round to the front of the vehicle and lifted it into place. 'Screw the nuts on finger tight, while I strap the damaged wheel into the back.'

He gave her the nuts, and she started to screw. The heat beat down on her, and perspiration trickled off her forehead into her eyes.

'Haven't you finished yet?' called Sven.

The last nut slipped out of Tay's perspiring fingers and dropped into the dust, and as she scrambled to retrieve it, her patience snapped.

'If you can do it any quicker yourself, go ahead!' She left the nut where it had fallen, and jumped resentfully to her feet.

Sven gave her a hard look, and bent to pick up the nut. He blew the dust from the threads and fitted it on to the bolt in one swift movement, then quickly applied his tool to bring all the nuts to a uniform tightness.

'Get back into your seat,' he ordered over his shoulder as he worked. 'I'll close the doors.'

If the force with which he slammed them was indicative of the state of his feelings, the next few hours promised to be fraught ones, Tay decided gloomily.

Lightning flickered through the windscreen as they resumed their hectic progress, and this time Tay caught the distant rumble of thunder, as if the elements, too, were at loggerheads with each other.

The heat grew more intense, pressing down on the battered earth like a great oppressive weight, and Tay blessed the opportunity she had taken to bring along fresh clothes, as she felt those she had on sticking wetly to her skin.

The check-point provided sandwiches and cold drinks, as it had the day before, but this time Sven did not return to the camper to help her down after the marshals had stamped their time card. Instead, he took his sandwiches and drink, and strode straight over to the line of back-up vehicles, leaving her to her own devices.

The second camper was there, this time, she noticed, but she decided to ignore it. If Sven wanted to go without her, let him. She refused to trot after him like a meek puppy-dog.

She could see him deep in conversation with the mechanic, and soon the two men approached, rolling a spare wheel between them, which they proceeded to change for the damaged wheel. A quick check over the engine, the bonnet slammed down, and they were on the road again, but from Sven's grim-visaged look his chat with the mechanic had done little to lighten his mood.

'Is there any news of Ken?' Tay asked him, determined not to be intimidated by his attitude.

'Why didn't you come and ask for yourself?' he snapped. 'As a matter of fact, Ken's arm was broken in two places, and he's in plaster from his elbow to his fingers.'

'Poor Ken. No wonder it took for ever to find out what was wrong with the camper's engine,' Tay deliberately sniped at the ability of the Fielding mechanics.

'It took about half an hour to discover what was wrong,' Sven retorted in a tight voice. 'If the engine hadn't been started up first, it wouldn't have taken so long to put the matter right. As it was, the whole thing had to be stripped down and thoroughly flushed out.'

'Flushed out?' What on earth for?'

'Because someone had the witty idea of pouring sugar into the petrol tank,' he ground out. Tay gasped.

'Who on earth would do a stupid thing like that?'

'*You* tell *me*,' he suggested, stony-faced.

Did he think it was herself? Tay stared at him in open-mouthed astonishment.

'That's one thing you can't possibly blame me for,' she burst out. 'I'd be the last person to sabotage one of our own engines.'

'Who knows how a woman's mind works?' he sneered. He *did* think it was her.

'I can't imagine how *your* mind's working. What reason could I possible have to do a thing like that?'

'Maybe to put Fielding off buying the Hilliard engine for our camper?' he offered her one. 'You'd go to any lengths to prevent a merger taking place between our two companies.'

'You must be crazy,' Tay burst out. 'I haven't been near the showrooms, or the campers, today.'

'The sugar was put in the petrol tank some time in the night. The mechanic told me that the security guard heard a noise, and went to investigate, but he found nobody there, so he assumed it was a swinging door that somebody had left open.'

'I went to bed early, the night we arrived. I was tired.'

'You *say* you went to bed early,' Sven said significantly.

'You really believe I'd go to such lengths as sabotaging our own engine?'

'It fits,' clipped Sven.

'Of all the crazy, twisted reasoning ...' Sven's accusation was almost unbelievable. So, too, was his driving skill.

The impala buck leapt out of the bush right in front of them, fleeing from some nameless terror that pursued it from behind. Sven swerving violently. Rocks and stones scattering in all directions, flung up by the screaming wheels, that raised a mini dust-storm round them. Tay caught a flash of sun-bronzed coat, near to the colour of her own hair, graceful, curved horns and terror-stricken eyes.

With a mighty bound the buck cleared the camper's bonnet, and two dark rump markings registered the fact that it was past and heading into the distance.

'Did we touch him?' shouted Sven, his hands white-knuckled on the wheel as he fought to steady the wildly skidding camper.

'No, we missed him by inches.'

'Let's hope we gave him time to get safely away from whatever it was he was running from.'

Tay did not answer. She felt a sudden bond of kinship with the fleeing impala. She was herself running from something she could not identify, and failed to understand, but which was inexorably driving her into a corner, with no way out that she could see and no defence.

First, the episode of the stolen photograph. And now, the sugar in the petrol tank. Sven seemed determined to hold her responsible for both. And how could she prove that she was not?

In spite of the heat she shivered as she remembered his portentous words of last night.

'Those that hunt in silence are the ones to fear.'

But who was doing the hunting, and why?

A proud Masai stood statuesque beside the track to watch the camper flash by, his fierce-looking spear a sure defence against any lion that might hold ambitions to raid his large herd of cattle spread grazing across the plain nearby.

Tay frowned. She had no defence against a threat which she was at a loss to identify.

But the hazards of the terrain prevented her from brooding for too long. Another check-point. Another cool, welcome drink, but having it sitting in the cab this time, since only ten minutes break was allowed, and there was no time for Tay to get out and stretch her legs. And then on again, to where loose sand trapped their wheels, bogging them down in a deep gulley that the blazing sun had turned into a desert.

'Get out the sand-ladders, quickly, and put them under the wheels while I drive over them,' he ordered. Quick as a flash he released Tay's seat-harness himself, and she fled to do his bidding.

She dragged out the sand-ladders and slid them under the wheels, then flagged Sven forward, as he manoeuvred the camper on to them, and over the sand-trap. Then he stopped, and Tay retrieved the ladders and threw them back into the camper, and jumped back into her seat.

'Get going,' she called, as she buckled her harness back on.

'Look ahead of us!' Sven exulted. 'Number one's stuck too. Now's our chance!'

There was no time to lose. The other navigator had already got out his own sand-ladders, and his car was beginning to crawl over them. In another minute it would gather sufficient speed to become a renewed threat. Sven swung the camper round the car, seeking out every available inch of firm ground on which to give his tyres a grip.

A wake of sand streamed out behind each wheel. The tyres were wide, and provided a broad base to grip, but even so they floundered again, and Tay held her breath as she felt them begin to spin, but somehow Sven kept them going forward, inching their way through the sliding grains, and in another minute they gripped firm ground, and held.

'We're through!' triumphed Sven, and laughed delightedly across at Tay.

We . . .

The miniscule word linked them together, and acknowledged that Tay was of some use on the trip after all, that Sven could not, in fact, have got out of the sand by himself in time to pass the car in front.

We . . . Tay hugged the small concession to her. It was a grudging one, but it had the effect of putting her in a more cheerful frame of mind when she started to get out the cooking-equipment and supplies to make their supper at the night-stop shortly afterwards.

The huts were similar to the ones that had been provided on the previous night, but this time there were tall trees sheltering the huts, and, Tay saw with delight, they were populated. Families of baboons watched her every movement, with a fascination as strong as her own in theirs.

'We'll have a treat tonight,' she decided aloud. Some of her stiffness had worn off during the day, and cooking the supper did not seem such an impossible task tonight.

'Great,' Sven answered enthusiastically. 'I'm starving. What's it to be? Sardines, or beans?'

'A surprise,' she answered mysteriously. Even dry bread would taste good with Sven in a better temper.

She raided the cool-box and found tomatoes, eggs and fresh fruit. She piled them all together on one of the plates, and placed it handily in the doorway of the nearest hut. In a moment of abandon, she used the entire stock of fresh fruit, and balanced the inevitable long loaf on top at a crazy angle to suit her mood, then turned her attention to the stove.

She was kneeling beside it, working energetically with her back to the hut, when she heard Sven shout.

'Watch the food, Tay, for goodness' sake!'

Tay spun round in time to see their precious supplies disappearing under a writhing mass of baboons. They snarled and fought to try to grab the choicest pieces for themselves. No wonder they had watched what she was doing with such close attention!

'Go away! Shoo! Oh, you wretches!' she cried in dismay.

She jumped to her feet and ran at them, holding the empty saucepan threateningly aloft, and the baboons fled with their booty, shrieking and chattering. All except one. He was a particularly large male, and he stood his ground, facing her, his yellow fangs opened in a snarl.

'Keep your distance, Tay—he's dangerous!' called Sven.

She could hear his footsteps running towards her, and the next moment the saucepan was snatched out of her hand as he grabbed it and hurled it at the snarling animal, which bounded away and sought safety in the nearest tree.

'There goes our supper!' wailed Tay. 'I used all the fresh fruit and veg to make us a treat.'

'Some treat!' snarled Sven, with a look as ferocious as that of the baboon. 'That was our last loaf, as well. It's to be hoped you're not hungry. There's no chance of our getting any more supplies until we meet up with the back-up camper at midday tomorrow. That is, if its engine's still working by then,' he added savagely, and swinging on his heel; he stamped away to resume his task of checking the vehicle.

Tay surveyed the wreckage of their supper. The tin of sausages was intact. It had no obvious smell of food, so had not attracted the attentions of the marauders. Moodily, she checked the cool-box. It yielded one tin of sardines, and two tins of beans. The rest resembled Mother Hubbard's cupboard.

'You needn't sulk,' she protested as she meticulously shared the heated sausages, and the contents of one tin of beans, between herself and Sven. 'I wasn't to know the wretched creatures would descend on us like a swarm of locusts. I'd have thought they'd be too afraid of human beings to venture on to the ground.'

'You could have used a bit of common sense,' he blamed her. 'If you weren't so besotted with studying the animals, you'd have realised what a temptation the food must have been to them, leaving it in the hut doorway like that. They must have thought it was an open invitation to supper,' he snorted.

'If you're still hungry, you can have mine.' Angrily, Tay thrust her own plate towards him.

'Don't be silly. Eat it yourself. I've got enough,' he said, and thrust the plate aside.

'Then stop grumbling.'

'I'm not grumbling. I was only saying ...'

They were quarrelling again, quarrelling about the food, just the same as the baboons did, Tay thought, suddenly sickened, and found it difficult to force down the last few forkfuls of sausage and beans left on her plate.

He had virtually ignored her after supper, concentrating his whole attention on the route instructions for the following day, and without a great deal of success, Tay pretended to do the same with her own copy. Inexplicably, the printed words persisted in blurring in front of her eyes, until with a sigh of exasperation she eventually abandoned her fruitless efforts and took herself off to bed.

Sven responded to her, 'Good night,' with a brief, ''Night,' but he did not look up from his reading, and Tay stormed through her own undressing, and needed no bidding to turn her back on him when he came in later and prepared for bed himself.

She rolled over on to her back now and glared across at him, resenting the ease with which he could put the traumas of the day behind him and slip into merciful oblivion.

At the sight of him, her heart gave an unexpected twist. His unconscious face looked young and strangely vulnerable in sleep. The sight of Sven, recumbent and unaware, in the opposite bunk roused emotions in her that were deeper, and stronger, and definitely more disturbing than anything she had ever felt before.

She would not look at him, she decided quickly. If she could not see him, the feelings would go away.

She rolled over on to her side away from him, and shut her eyes tightly. And discovered to her dismay that a clear image of his sleeping face remained firmly beneath her closed lids, refusing to go away.

Which disturbed her even more.

CHAPTER SIX

THEIR sparse breakfast the next morning did nothing to lighten the atmosphere between them. Even the generous restocking of their cool-box from the back-up camper at lunchtime made no difference to Sven's aloof disapproval, and Tay writhed under the sheer injustice of his attitude.

The brooding storm, heightening the humidity, combined to make matters worse, and by the end of the fourth day, heat and dehydration brought Tay to the end of her tether. The jolts and jars and skids of the tracks, the dust and flies and mosquitoes, seemed as if they would go on for ever, like some dreadful punishment being inflicted upon her, although for what, she had no idea.

Sven would give her two excellent reasons. And he would be wrong—so wrong.

She map-read with eyes that were glazed by dust and weariness, and once she missed a vital turning.

'Go back,' she cried urgently to Sven. 'We should have taken the track *before* the fork, not the one after it.'

Tight-lipped, Sven swung the camper round, and roared back to the almost invisible track indicated on the map.

'That's lost us three whole minutes, thanks to you!' he shouted at her.

'*Only* three minutes!' Tay shouted back, refusing to regard it as the end of the world. 'Anyone can make mistakes in terrain as bad as this!'

She was angry with Sven for shouting at her, angry with herself, for giving him the opportunity.

'We'll lose points for this,' he snapped. 'It could lose us our place.'

He would never forgive her if it did. Would she ever forgive herself?

'Put your foot down, and make up the time.' She thrust the onus back on to him.

The last section of all was the worst.

'The Trials route's notoriously bad from here back to the finish, Miss Hilliard,' the mechanic from the back-up vehicle warned her worriedly at the morning stop. 'Let me change places with you. You could drive the little camper back to Nairobi quite easily. It's a tarmac road all the way. I'd go with Mr Diamond.'

'Tay insisted on coming, so she can stay the rest of the course,' Sven cut the mechanic short. 'That is, unless you want to chicken out?' He swung round and eyed Tay challengingly.

'Wouldn't you just love me to do that?' she jeered, and swinging on her heel she marched purposefully round the camper and clambered back on board, slamming the door behind her like an exclamation mark.

With her back towards Sven, she did not see the sudden glint that flashed deep in his blue eyes, and it was gone when he turned to speak to the mechanic before joining her in the cab, and roaring away in obedience to the officiating marshal's signal.

The electric storm broke halfway through the afternoon.

Flashes of lightning lit the sky in a continuous natural firework display, accompanied by great crashes of thunder. The deluge hit them suddenly. A great wall of rain descended from the sky and hissed into the parched ground. Steam rose round them, turning the track into a cauldron, and the wheels slid on ochre-coloured mud that seconds before had been inches of dry dust.

Streams of water double-glazed the windscreen until it was impossible to see through it clearly, and the dry watercourse they had crossed on the way out was turned into a torrent by the time they reached it.

'Wait until the rain eases off a bit,' cried Tay, staring aghast at the brown water swirling round the rocks at the bottom of the watercourse.

'I daren't,' Sven retorted. 'It's getting deeper every minute. The storm could go on for hours yet. If we wait for the rain to stop, the watercourse could become impassable.'

It hurtled noisily into the surrounding bushland, where Tay could hear it crashing its way along the dried-up bed long after it vanished from sight.

'The camper's built high off the ground. You'll be able to see better when it's stopped raining.'

'The camper isn't amphibious,' he reminded her. 'We've still got to climb out on the other side. It's a good job the far bank isn't so steep as this one. If we can get there before the mud becomes too deep, we should be able to climb out while the wheels still have something firm to grip on underneath.'

The tyres found precious little purchase on the bank confronting them. Sven eased the camper cautiously over the edge, but the tyres floundered and spun on the greasy surface, and carried them downwards in a slithering rush which took rocks and mud and debris along with them to the bottom.

The front wheels dived into the water up to their hub caps, and when the back wheels followed suit, the torrent caught at them with a force out of all proportion to its depth.

'The back's swinging round!' Tay cried.

It stopped with a sickening crunch against something hard and unyielding lying on the river bed. Sven revved the engine hard, but the camper did not move.

'We're jammed,' he frowned, 'Take over the wheel, while I get out and put my shoulder against the side. I may be able to rock us free.'

He was out of the doorway in a flash, and wading round to the back of the camper, and Tay saw with horror that the water came nearly up to his waist.

'Slip into gear, and rev up when I signal,' he called back, and she waved a hand to show that she understood.

She craned out of the window, and watched as Sven bent down and applied his shoulder to the back of the vehicle. It took three mighty heaves before the laden camper moved. Tay felt the vehicle rock. Sven's arm rose in an urgent signal, and she let in the clutch and revved madly.

'Keep going,' Sven called.

She could see his hand through the door mirror, urging her on, and with gritted teeth she put her foot hard on the accelerator, and steered for the opposite bank. The front wheels touched it, and held, and the camper lurched out of the river like a hippopotamus from its wallow, shedding water and debris as it went.

Tay glanced triumphantly behind her, just in time to see Sven fall. He stumbled over something hidden below the muddy water, and with flailing arms, he fell full length into the torrent, with a mighty splash.

Tay laughed out loud. 'That'll cool his temper,' she chuckled.

Her laugh died as suddenly as it came. Sven broke surface with one hand clutching at his opposite shoulder, and staggered unsteadily in the wake of the camper, his arm hanging limply at his side.

Heedless of his order to keep going, Tay slammed on the brakes and killed the engine, and raced down the bank towards him. Blood was beginning to send a dark streak down his shirt, and his face was grey as he groaned.

'I landed on a boulder underneath the water. My arm's gone numb. You'll have to drive the rest of the way.'

The route back to Nairobi was a nightmare which was to haunt Tay for a long time to come.

She drove like one possessd. Her desire to prove herself to Sven vanished. Nothing mattered now except the overriding need to get Sven to medical attention quickly.

She was conscious of a searing agony in her arms as she fought the wildly bucking wheel along the worst and most dangerous section of the whole Trials route, of Sven, reaching out his good hand, and closing it over her own, lending her his strength on the worst places, where her own was not enough. Of the crooked grin which creased his dirt-streaked face, that mouthed, 'Great girl! Keep going. You're doing fine,' giving her the strength of Hercules just when her own threatened to give out.

A singing exultation raced through her veins at his praise, and there was no hazard on earth she would not have tackled, reinforced by that special grin from Sven, special for her alone.

It took her at top speed into the final check-point in the hotel car park at Nairobi, scattering the marshals. She slammed on the brakes and thrust the time-card through the window into their waiting hands. She called out urgently, 'Look after Sven, somebody. He's hurt,' and leaned limply across the steering-wheel, her strength spent.

Arms reached into the camper and lifted her down from her seat. Ken Wallace's arms. She saw that one of them was encased in plaster. Somebody else was helping Sven out on the opposite side. 'You've done wonderful, Miss Tay,' Ken Wallace praised her. 'You should stand a chance of coming in the first three.'

But Tay no longer cared. The only result she was interested in was an X-ray of Sven's shoulder.

'Sven?' She tried to push her way through the crowd that surrounded him, but her slight figure made no impression on the crush of burly newsmen all crowding to take his picture, and somebody else reached him first.

'Sven, *darling*!' It was Olive.

Cameras whirred, and flash-bulbs popped in Tay's face. The press and television were out in force to greet the returning competitors. She thought wretchedly, 'I must look a complete mess.'

Olive looked superb. She was fresh, and cool, and sophisticated, in flawless fondant-green linen, with her hair piled high, and her favourite perfume an exotic cloud around her. She latched on to Sven as if she had got sole rights over him.

Like a racehorse owner leading in a Derby winner, Tay thought sourly, watching with a scowl as Olive's varnished nails rested on Sven's arm in a proprietorial gesture.

She herself felt filthy, smelly, and exhausted, and wished only that the cameras would point the other way until she had time to repair the ravages that would show up starkly on any photograph, and make Olive positively purr with pleasure at the contrast.

Tay gave up the unequal contest with a shrug, and begged Ken Wallace, 'Can't you rescue him, Ken? Sven's hurt his shoulder. His arm's useless. He ought to see a doctor.'

She felt a stab of surprise at the extremity of her anxiety for Sven. Did spending four traumatic days and nights with a man do this sort of thing to a person? she wondered, and exploded into action to avoid having to answer her own unanswerable question.

'Leave the interviews until later,' she pleaded with the reporters, raising her voice anxiously over the hubbub to make them listen to her. 'Sven's hurt his arm.'

'The lady must be good medicine for him,' one of the reporters laughed. 'He seems to be making a quick recovery.'

Clearly, he was. The arm that had hung limp and useless when Sven emerged from the river was now circling Olive's waist. drawing the two of them close together to face the battery of cameras. Another grin creased Sven's face now, but it was beamed on Olive this time, with Tay forgotten.

Flaunting themselves, Tay condemned them wrathfully to herself, and felt suddenly sick.

Had Sven deliberately exaggerated the extent of his injury in order to load the driving on to her on the last, and worst, section of the Trials route? Opting out, in order to punish her for insisting upon taking Ken Wallace's place?

Worse still, had he done it to give himself a handy scapegoat, in case they did not come first?

Sven already blamed her in his own mind for the leaked photograph and the sabotage of the camper's engine. Did he, coward-like, want to hold her in reserve, to vindicate his own performance if they lost the Trials? Scott Fielding was not a man to tolerate a loser, and it would weigh heavily against Sven in the power struggle for succession between himself and Lance if he failed in his chairman's eyes.

'I'm going to get cleaned up,' she told Ken Wallace quickly, and ignoring his surprised, 'Won't the reporters want some more photographs of you, Miss Tay?' she battled her way through the gaggle of newsmen towards the hotel.

She met Lance, battling in the opposite direction. He was carrying a fondant-green linen something in his hand.

'I've missed the first cars coming in,' he grumbled. 'Olive wanted me to fetch her the jacket to her dress, though goodness knows why she wants a jacket on in this heat.'

Tay could have told him. It was a neat ploy to get Lance out of the way while Olive hogged the limelight with Sven. She felt strongly tempted to tell him so. He had not seen the two of them together, yet, because of the crush. But he would find out soon enough, because just then Sven's voice rang out above the noise of the crowd.

'Tay? You're wanted!'

Tay left Lance standing, and fled up the hotel steps. Sven did not want her along with him in the Trials, so he could do without her now.

Now, he had got Olive.

The sudden stinging of her eyes took her by surprise, and she blinked hastily and hurried upstairs, her face averted in case one of the sharp-eyed reporters should notice.

'I must be more tired than I thought,' she discovered, dismayed. Tears were not a weakness she was prone to.

The weariness dropped from her like a sloughed skin as she bathed away the dirt and the grime of the journey, and she wallowed in the warm, scented water, letting it draw out the bumps and the bruises, the resentments and the aches, and the anger, of the last few hectic days.

And discovered, as she wrapped herself in her robe afterwards, and dropped gratefully on to her soft bed, that it had no power to wash away the unexpected ache that still remained like a leaden weight inside her.

It was still there when she awoke some time later. Its presence made swallowing food out of the question, and the prospect of remaining alone in her room untenable. Her father was still in Mombasa. He would not be back until tomorrow, in time for the celebration dinner and ball, at which the winner of the Trials would be announced and receive the coverted silver trophy. Ken Wallace was keeping an appointment at the local hospital to have his new plaster checked for comfort and might not be back yet, so she could not rely on him for company.

Shopping held no appeal, and she did not want to go walking on her own. She searched uninterestingly through her clothing for something to put on, and came across her swimsuit.

'Just the thing!' she exclaimed. Swimming was an occupation which she could enjoy without the need of a companion, and the hotel boasted a superb pool.

Swiftly she slipped into her costume, and slinging a matching wrap carelessly over her shoulder, she ran outside to where groups of inviting-looking chairs and loungers lined the cool tiling at the poolside.

Only two of them were in use, and their occupants looked up and saw Tay before she could retreat. Olive eyed her up and down insolently, and she forced herself to walk towards them, pinning a determined smile on her lips as she went.

'How's your shoulder?' she asked Sven casually, as if it were a mere trifle that she only mentioned out of politeness, and tried to hide her anxiety even from herself as she waited for him to reply.

It was badly bruised, she could see that. There was a cut where it had bled, but the water must have spread the stain across his shirt and made the bleeding seem worse than it was, because the cut did not look as if it was particularly deep. Tay dropped into one of the poolside chairs, hiding her rush of relief as Sven said,

'Nothing's broken. I've had it X-rayed.'

His eyes narrowed against the light, so that she could not read their expression as he added, 'Apparently when I banged it against the boulder as I fell, the blow temporarily numbed a nerve. I've got the use back in my arm again now.'

He had put it to excellent use, encircling Olive's waist.

'It'll probably be stiff tomorrow,' Tay opined.

'I've been told to use it, to minimise the stiffness.'

No doubt he would use it again in the same way, to his satisfaction and Olive's

The other girl's black eyes jeered at Tay from where she lay stretched at full length on her lounger. Her even, all-over tan betrayed the hours she must have spent in the same position acquiring it, shown off to advantage by the brief aquamarine bikini that she wore.

Not that Sven seemed to object to Olive's attire, or the lack of it.

'Rub some lotion on my shoulders for me, there's a darling,' Olive pleaded with him prettily, stretching up her hand to give him the bottle.

She slanted a triumphant upward glance at Tay as Sven obligingly took the lotion from her, and bade her accommodatingly, 'Turn over, then.'

Nothing could have been more calculated to suggest a close intimacy between the two, or to make Tay feel more of an intruder. Viewed dispassionately, it made a charming poolside scene.

Except that Olive was married to Lance.

Where did Sven fit into the picture? Tay wondered, and was shocked by the hot anger that shook her at what must be the only answer.

She could watch the charade no longer.

'I'm going to have a swim,' she announced abruptly. Dropping her wrap on to her chair she ran to the water's edge and, touching the tips of her fingers together in a neat point above her head, she dived, cleaving the water cleanly without a splash.

The cool depths of it closed over her head, shutting her off from the world. Shutting out Olive and Sven. Tay felt scorched by the heat of her anger against them. There was no reason why their actions should concern her. They were both adults, and their behaviour was none of her business.

But a deep sense of betrayal for which she could not account added to the force of her fury, and drove her at speed across the pool, making for the other side, putting as much distance between herself and the other two as she possibly could.

The green tiles of the further side closed in on her, and she reached up for the grab rail to haul herself out of the water.

'Did you *have* to snub the journalists like that, when we

got in this morning?' Sven demanded from behind her.

Tay whipped round, startled. She had no idea he was swimming behind her. He must have left Olive's side to follow her, almost at the same instant as she dived into the pool.

Which would upset Olive, Tay thought with vindictive satisfaction, and she eyed Sven warily.

He must be an expert swimmer, to make so little sound when he entered the water that the splash did not alert her. And a fast one, too, to enable him to catch up with her so easily. She was no slouch herself with her overarm stroke, and fury had driven her across the pool at twice her usual speed.

With an effort she recovered from her surprise, and parried, 'Like what? They'd got enough photographs of me to fill an album when I left. Anyway, they took enough pictures of you and Olive by the camper to satisfy a dozen news editors,' Tay said unguardedly.

'Jealous?' taunted Sven, and Tay's eyes snapped.

'Jealous of what?' she cried insultingly.

They were quarrelling again, and this time it was about Olive. Suddenly Tay could not bear it. With an eel-like wriggle she slipped back into the water, and sped away from Sven. But before she had gone more than a couple of feet he caught up with her and reached out to grasp her arm as she swam.

Quick as a flash Tay dived, and went under water. Twisting and turning, she swam below him to confuse him, but with lightning reaction Sven divined her intention, and in seconds he was beside her again, and this time, when he reached out his hand, he caught her easily. With a quick tug he pulled her close, and his lips came down on hers in a crushing kiss that bound her to him as they rose through the water together.

'You ...' They surfaced, and drew apart, and Tay's anger spilled over. Her hand came back.

'It's time someone cooled you down,' gritted Sven.

He parried her blow easily, then, still holding her hand, he dived. Tay had only just time to gulp in a quick lungful of air before she found herself dragged beneath the surface and towed along behind Sven towards the deep end of the pool by the diving-board.

'What are you trying to do, drown me?' she spluttered, fighting for air after an aeon of time when she thought Sven would never surface.

'You tempt me strangely, Copper,' he returned, and there was something in his eyes and his voice that brought hot colour flooding to her cheeks.

'Go away and leave me alone!' she cried, wrenching her arm free from his hold. 'I'm tired of being shouted at by you. Go back to Olive. If you don't go soon, you'll find your place has been taken!'

None too soon, so far as Tay was concerned, someone else had been attracted to the poolside. A camera-hung individual was deep in conversation with Olive. He turned, and Tay saw that it was the ferret-faced reporter who had approached her earlier.

'But of course, Mr Diamond and I know each other *very* well,' Olive was saying. Her words carried to Tay and Sven clearly across the water, accompanied by her high-pitched, tinkling laugh.

Sven swore suddenly under his breath. 'It's your pal again,' he snarled at Tay.

'Confessions of a director's wife?' She ignored his snide reference. 'They should make an interesting story,' she remarked nastily.

'If you've put that reporter up to this, I'll make you pay for it,' Sven threatened, and before Tay's startled mind had time to grasp what he meant, he was already across the pool, skimming through the water towards Olive and the reporter, Tay saw thoughtfully, as if he were competing for the Blue Riband.

Clearly, he meant to intervene before Olive had an opportunity to say any more, and his urgency served to confirm what she already suspected lay between the two. Her expression hardened.

No matter what Sven thought, she had no hand in the reporter's presence. But it would serve Sven right if the affair *was* made public. If Olive bared their guilty secret to the reporter, it would not only interest the newspaper's readers, it would also interest Lance, which explained Sven's haste now. If Olive did not mind her husband knowing, Sven obviously did. Tay drifted across the pool towards the little group, drawn by a compelling need to find out how he would cope with the situation.

'What do you want with Mrs Poulton?' Sven asked the reporter roughly, as he vaulted up on to the tiled poolside.

From the dismay on the ferrety face, it was obvious the man had thought Olive to be on her own, and had been emboldened to approach her because of that. Sven's emergence from the water must have seemed like the wrath of Neptune, Tay thought with a grin.

'I only want a bit of background blurb, Mr Diamond,' the man said with an ingratiating smile. 'Human-interest sort of material, to please our readers.' His smile turned into a leer.

'Clear off,' Sven ordered brusquely. 'Come on, Olive.'

Leaning down, he took hold of Olive's hand and pulled her up abruptly from the lounger on to her feet.

'Don't be so rough, darling.' she protested, pouting prettily. 'You're usually so gentle.'

It was beautifully done. It said nothing, and everything. Almost Tay could admire her opportunism.

Olive's next move said even more, without the need of words. As Sven pulled her to her feet, she slipped, or pretended to, and fell against him. Instinctively he raised his arms to catch her, and in a flash the reporter pointed his camera and snapped them both neatly, with Olive laughing up into Sven's face, and her arms clinging to his broad shoulders.

It was the sort of picture that might be produced as evidence in a divorce court.

Sven was not looking at the reporter when it was taken. He was looking down into Olive's face. But although the sound of the shutter was only a slight click, his keen ears detected it. With a move so swift that Olive could hardly have been aware of what he was doing, he caught her clinging hands and thrust them away from him, and spun to face the reporter.

The man had no time to back out of reach. One minute he had his camera in his own hands, and the next it was transferred magically to Sven's. With vicious fingers Sven wrenched it open and extracted the film, and flung it angrily over his shoulder towards the pool.

'That's got rid of that!' he grated.

'Not quite,' Tay said coolly, and fielded the missile with a neatness of which even her cricket-mad father would approve.

She did not know what made her catch the film. Privately, she agreed with Sven's sentiments. She did not like the film, or its unpleasant owner, and thought that both would benefit from a ducking.

But she caught it just the same, on an obscure impulse to punish Sven somehow, for his behaviour with Olive.

''Ere, that film belongs to me! Give it back!' the reporter shouted, hastening to the poolside.

'I'll think about it.' Cautiously, Tay slid further out into the pool, out of reach, carefully holding the cassette well clear of the water.

'It's got all my pictures of the Trials on it, that film has,' the man blustered. 'It's more than my job's worth to go back to the office without them.'

'It'll be more than your life's worth, if you print any of your scurrilous articles about me,' Sven told him, and advanced menacingly.

The reporter backed away, changing his tactics.

'Speak to him, will you, miss?' he pleaded with Tay.

'You know him well. You can make him see ...'

'I don't know him all that well,' Tay denied, and added sweetly, 'I've only spent the last four nights with him.'

Viewed objectively, the expressions on the three faces turned towards her from the poolside should have been hysterically funny.

So why did she suddenly want to weep?

She heard Olive's outraged gasp, as she flounced back towards the hotel, saw the reporter's mouth open, and then close, before he scuttled like a rabbit in Olive's wake, choosing to retreat rather than remain alone with Sven's wrath at the poolside.

That's given him something new to think about, Tay thought, but curiously her bull's-eye gave her little satisfaction.

The black fury on Sven's face made her wish suddenly that she were somewhere else, a long way off. He sprang off the tiles with a mighty leap that sent his body arcing towards her like an avenging arrow.

Tay saw him coming, and turned to flee, but as well try to escape a lightning bolt as try to get away from Sven's vengeance. He hit the water and in two strokes she was his captive.

Hard fingers closed round her wrists in a merciless grip, and he wrenched her arms behind her back with a force that made her hands go numb. Limply, her fingers opened and loosed the film, which drifted slowly, and unheeded, to the bottom of the pool.

'Let me go,' she gasped. 'The reporter might be still watching us.'

'Why should I care about your reputation, when you don't seem to care about it yourself?' snarled Sven. 'You've just given that fellow enough material to make three-inch headlines in the gutter press.' Deliberately, he bent her backwards under him in the water.

'I suppose you think, if he writes about me, he'll leave you and Olive alone?' Tay taunted.

'I ought to slap you for that,' Sven snarled. 'But come to think of it, it isn't a bad idea to give him some worthwhile copy!'

If the reporter was still watching, Sven gave him plenty to write about. Tay was helpless to stem the onslaught of his anger, and his lips inflicted harsh punishment on hers that she could do nothing to escape.

She held herself rigid in his grasp, enduring his cruelty that became greater still when, after a lifetime of punishment, his lips suddenly forwent their harshness and softened, coaxing a response from her own. They nuzzled against her mouth, parting its soft contours, and his arms moved too, cradling her against him, while his hands caressed her shoulders, and his legs worked, lazily propelling them together across the surface of the pool.

'Are you sorry?' he demanded.

Was she sorry?

Tay's mind tried to fight him. But against her will, she felt herself beginning to relax, responding to the silent enticement of their slow drift through the water.

Without conscious volition on her part, her body began to mould itself instictively to his movements, and feeling her response, Sven's tongue reached out and flicked lazily across her lips, reawakening all the nameless longings that had stirred in her on the night he held her in his arms in the camper. Slowly, they drifted nearer to the steps that led out of the pool.

Was she sorry?

Sven's kisses were a trap, snaring her senses. His stroking hands were an invitation, tempting her to give in, and allow the longings to surface, giving him kiss for passionate kiss.

And hand to the watching reporter a story that would make him forget all about Sven and Olive.

With a violent contortion, Tay lunged away from him, breaking free from his arms.

Her feet came into contact with the bottom of the

steps, and swiftly she turned and climbed them, scrambling on hands and knees in her haste to get away from Sven. She reached the top and turned, glaring down at him in the water, her face filled with loathing for him, and for herself.

'No, I'm not sorry,' she spat. 'Not now—not ever!'

She choked to a halt, and spinning away, she ran for the hotel, uncaring whether or not the reporter might be watching. She was desperate only to get away from Sven, before the hidden, nameless longings rose to the surface and named themselves. And made her very, very sorry indeed.

Because if she allowed that to happen, she would have walked blindly right into the trap that Scott Fielding and Sven between them had dug for her for that very purpose.

CHAPTER SEVEN

DINNER that night brought an unexpected olive-branch from Sven.

Tay descended hungrily to the dining-room. 'It'll be a treat to eat a decent meal again,' she confided to Ken Wallace on the way down. 'Sardines are all very well in their place, but after a steady diet of them for four days . . .' She took the menu from the waiter.

The hors d'oeuvres was sardines.

However skilfully disguised and cunningly labelled, the ubiquitous fish remained. Tay stared balefully at the printed offering. And then, as if drawn by a magnet, her eyes flew up and found Sven's face, and they both burst out laughing.

To her surprise, Sven came round to her chair between courses, and invited her to dance with him on the small, cleared area of the room that would later hold a floor-show. She could hardly refuse without causing comment, and she rose reluctantly.

'How about declaring an armistice, Copper?' he asked unexpectedly as they circled the floor to the strains of the instrumentalists discreetly tucked away in a palm-decorated corner.

Tay looked her astonishment, and he added with a crooked smile, 'Only until after the celebration dinner's over tomorrow evening. You can pick up the cudgels again then, if you want to. But we're supposed to be a team, remember? The press will expect us to show a united front at the dinner tomorrow evening.'

Was this his only reason for suggesting an armistice? Simply as a façade to present to the press? Or was her fiery reaction to his advances making it more difficult

111

than he had anticipated to carry out Scott's instructions?

Whatever his reason, it was a thorn well hidden in his olive-branch, but in spite of the risk of getting scratched, Tay found herself reaching out for it cautiously.

Despite the colour of her hair, quarrelling was alien to her nature, and she found her abrasive relationship with Sven so far a distinct strain. Even surface politeness would be better than nothing for the few days they had still left in Kenya. After that, she need never see him again.

A grey cloud of depression enveloped her at the thought, and she broke into speech, fearful lest her feelings should show in her face, and betray her.

'We'll call a truce, if you want to,' she answered guardedly.

'As from now,' he agreed, and steered her back to the table, to resume their interrupted meal, as if that had been the sole reason he had asked her to dance in the first place, and now that he had got his way, he no longer wanted to go on dancing with her.

As soon as the meal was over, Tay pleaded weariness and excused herself, and Sven did the same, disregarding Olive's protests at his early withdrawal.

'Tay and I have had an exhausting four days,' he reminded her.

An imp inside Tay felt tempted to add, 'And nights,' but after her experience of Sven's reaction in the swimming-pool she did not quite dare, and submitted to his hand cupping her elbow, conscious of Olive's vitriolic stare as Sven guided her out of the room.

He stopped at the doorway of her room. 'Good night, Copper,' he murmured. He lowered his head, and his kiss lingered, setting the seal on their armistice for however short a time it might last.

His lips clung to Tay's mouth, and although she knew she must break away, for some reason—perhaps it was tiredness?—she did not try. When at last Sven freed her, she stood looking up at him in silence, and he repeated with a smile, 'Good night, Copper,' and turned her towards her door.

'Good night,' she stammered, and stumbling through into her room she shut the door behind her, leaned against it and closed her eyes, and knew a strange, aching hunger inside her that could not be satisfied with food.

She got up very early the next morning and hastened downstairs, intent on exploring while it was still reasonably cool.

Sven was waiting for her. He leaned negligently against the newel-post, swinging two racquets in his hand as she came downstairs.

'Tennis?' she queried.

'The hotel's got a super court. Haven't you seen it?' When she shook her head he said, 'I've booked it for the first hour, I thought you'd like a game of tennis before it gets too hot.'

Tay felt tempted. It was a long time since she had enjoyed a really good game of tennis, but,

'Weren't you planning to play with Olive?'

'At this time in the morning?' jeered Sven. 'You don't know Olive very well.'

Tay did not want to, but she let it pass.

'She won't be up until at least eleven o'clock, if then,' Sven predicted. He seemed to have an intimate knowledge of Olive's personal habits.

'I was going to explore,' Tay hedged.

'Tennis first, and explore afterwards,' Sven decided. 'I'll take you the rounds of all the interesting places myself,' he added magnanimously.

'I can't resist the offer.' Tay was stung into forgetting the truce between them.

'Good,' he responded, smiling. 'Now let's see if your tennis is any better than your driving.'

'You were glad enough for me to drive yesterday,' she threw back at him defensively. 'It was along the worst part of the route, too.' Now she could remind him, and she availed herself of the opportunity with relish.

'*In extremis.*'

'Beast!' she hissed, and swung her racquet as if she would like to use it against Sven instead of the balls, as she took her place opposite to him on the court.

'Let's have a knockabout first, to get each other's measure before we begin to play in earnest,' he suggested, and lobbed a ball at her across the net.

She vented her anger on the spinning white globe, hitting it with force, regardless of where it would land.

Sven caught the ball in mid-air with a hard, back-hand swipe. It left his racquet with a velocity that made Tay gasp. She almost ducked, and recovered her courage just in time.

She needed both hands on her racquet to withstand the force of the shot. Even so, when the ball hit the gut, it almost knocked the handle out of her hands, but somehow she managed to return it. More by luck than good judgement, it landed just inside the line on the opposite side of the court, making Sven race to return it.

'I'll make you run,' Tay threatened from across the net.

But in the game that followed, it was Tay herself who did most of the running. Sven dropped his balls strategically in a manner that kept her feet flying across the court until at last, out of sheer exhaustion, she was compelled to allow the last one to bounce out of her reach unchallenged.

'Game to me,' triumphed Sven.

Tay collapsed crossly on to a seat at the edge of the court, and accused him, 'You deliberately tried to wear me out. My shirt's wringing wet!'

'It's one way of keeping you out of mischief.' He dropped down on to the seat beside her with an unrepentant grin. 'Trot upstairs and get showered and changed, and we'll go and explore now. We can breakfast out, at a place I know.'

The excited anticipation that gripped Tay as she got ready was childish and quite irrational. It was dangerous, too, a small voice inside her warned darkly, but she ignored it, and donned her favourite dress in buttercup yellow to match her mood, with sandals of the same bright shade.

'Nice,' Sven approved, his eyes running over her as she came towards him in the hotel lobby ten minutes later, and Tay's cheeks warmed at his compliment.

Knowing Sven's reason for wanting to accompany her, it was madness to feel so happy. But it was a sweet madness, to pretend for just a short time that the reason did not exist, and to live in the pleasure of the present, strolling hand in hand with Sven in the cool of the early morning, as they set out together to explore the strange new city just awakening round them, whose beauties Sven had promised to unveil for her delight.

Tay quickly deduced, 'You know Nairobi well.'

'I was assigned here for a while, a few years ago. It's a wonderful country,' he replied. 'I made a lot of friends during the two years I lived here.'

'There won't be time for me to do that,' said Tay, unconsciously wistful. 'We've only got three more days before we go home. I haven't even seen the animals in the game reserve properly,' she mourned.

'You will,' Sven promised her. 'I've arranged for us all to have a trip through the National Park tomorrow. You'll see all the wild animals then that you want to.'

'Do you really mean it?' she turned astonished eyes on him. 'But what about the business enquiries we've had? There won't be time for a whole day.'

'We're all having the day off from business,' Sven assured her. 'Your father's coming, and so is Scott. Even Andrew's joining us,' he added, with just the suspicion of a quirk to his well cut lips.

Scott Fielding must want the merger very badly to take

a day off from work, particularly for such an outing, Tay decided drily.

She thrust the thought from her. She would not allow it to spoil an experience that she always dreamed about, and when Sven quizzed her lightly, 'Are you pleased, Copper?' she replied with absolute truth, 'I'm over the moon.'

Big-game viewing was something she had always longed to do, and she thrust aside her forebodings as she strolled beside Sven past exclusive shops that held the sort of clothes Olive would delight in.

It was much too early as yet for them to be open and she gave the temptingly dressed windows hardly a glance, and sensing her lack of interest, Sven guided her on past them, to where he seemed to know by instinct she wanted to go.

The markets were a hive of activity. They rummaged happily together among the stalls, entranced by the endless variety and bustling life, thrilled to be a part of it themselves, until Tay completely lost count of time.

She bought a wood-carving for her father's study, but was too shy to haggle over the price. Sven did it for her, and she watched fascinated while he and the stallholder spent a mutually enjoyable five minutes arguing, and ended by striking a bargain that made them both happy.

Then they wandered on, admiring finely woven baskets and shapely pottery and stalls of brightly coloured cottons and trinkets. Sven purchased a bangle and slipped it on Tay's arm.

'It exactly matches the colour of your dress,' he excused his gift.

He loaded her arms with a rainbow of flowers as well, and then bought her a bright kerchief for her head when she admired the gay colours of those worn by the other women in the market.

He tied it on for her, because her arms were too full of flowers to allow her to do it for herself.

When he had settled the kerchief to his satisfaction, knotting it neatly at the back of her head, Sven ran his fingers on downwards along her spine, sending vibrations through the length of it that the expression in his eyes redoubled, as Tay's flew upwards, startled, to meet his teasing look.

'Breakfast,' he declared, his blue glance mocking her fiery blush, and in no time it seemed they left the bustle of the markets behind them and were seated in the cool shade of a garden.

Sven ordered their breakfast, and in a short time a platter of delicately spiced meats was placed before them, accompanied by various steaming dishes that she could not name but which tasted delicious, vying with their tempting aroma with the perfume of the exotic flowering bushes that turned the garden into a paradise of colour and scent.

There is something about breakfast, eaten piping hot in the open air, that makes it taste like no other meal on earth. And when it is rounded off with freshly cut pineapple sticks, probably one of the very pineapples they had seen at the market earlier, with juice that ran down her fingers as she nibbled, and lashings of steaming, aromatic coffee . . .

'This is bliss,' Tay sighed. And wondered with a pang of unease if the bliss sprang more from the fact that she was sharing the feast with Sven than from the food itself.

Sven ate his meal in near silence. He seemed suddenly preoccupied, as if his thoughts dwelt elsewhere, and Tay forbore to interrupt them, unwilling to spoil the rosy glow of the morning so far.

Once out of the shade of the garden, however, after their meal was over, she discovered that the heat had increased to enervating levels. Their journey of exploration had taken them longer than either of them had realised, and Sven hailed a taxi to return them to their hotel.

During the short drive back to the hotel, Tay was herself quiet and thoughtful, wrestling with the conundrum of her own wayward emotions which had suddenly risen to confront her, and which were still unresolved when they walked into the hotel lobby together.

Olive was there, sitting restlessly flicking over the pages of a glossy magazine. She looked up immediately Tay and Sven came in, as if she had been waiting for them.

'Where have you been?' she demanded. 'Scott's been looking all over for you!'

'Out,' Sven returned briefly.

Tay nearly added, 'Working.'

Which would have been true. All the morning, Sven had squired her, and fed her, and gifted her. And the mention of Scott's name reminded her that he had done so under orders from his Chairman. Her pleasure in the morning turned sour.

'You look like a gypsy, with that scarf thing on your head,' Olive told her rudely, and Tay snatched it off.

'I wanted some protection from the sun.' She felt she would have dearly loved to drop the scarf that had so attracted her into the nearest waste-bin, likewise the flowers, to show Sven how little his gifts meant to her.

Sven was nowhere in evidence when she went downstairs. He was probably still closeted with Scott, she surmised, but the hotel was full to overflowing with competition teams and journalists, all intent, now the serious business of the Trials was over, in enjoying their stay in Keyna to the full, and their bright, hail-fellow-well-met cheerfulness carried Tay along with it, until it was time to change for the celebration dinner.

Her dress was a rich ivory silk, the bodice softly bloused, and ending in a wide sash that tied in the front, and fell to one side halfway down the flowing skirt.

Her only adornment was a heavy choker of pearls, which toned in softly with the muted shade of her dress and matched her pearl-encrusted evening bag, and the pearl-studded heels of her tiny evening slippers.

A sharp tap sounded on her bedroom door as she neared the end of her toilet, and she called an abstracted, 'Come in,' as she raised her arms to fix the pearl choker in position. The necklet was new and the unaccustomed clasp was stiff, and Tay frowned at her reflection in the mirror as her fingers struggled in vain to unite the two ends. 'Would you tighten my choker for me, please?' she asked the incomer, assuming it was the maid.

'With pleasure,' Sven agreed, with weighted emphasis.

He strode across the room and came to a halt behind her, and Tay froze as he raised his hands and took the choker out of her suddenly nerveless fingers, and asked amusedly,

'Is there a lead that clips on to this collar thing, as well?'

'No, there isn't.' Indignantly, she whipped round to face him, fogetting that he still held the choker in his hands.

'Pity,' he commented. 'It'd be an excellent way of keeping you in order.'

'You . . .'

'Sit still,' he commanded. 'That is, if you want this confounded thing fastened up.' He checked her angry movement with a heavy hand on her shoulder.

'Don't bother,' Tay tried ineffectually to shrug away from under his grasp, 'I'll go without it.'

'It's fastened now.' Sven loosed her shoulder and deftly pushed the diamanté clip home on its fellow. 'It'll take you half the night to undo that fiddling litle clip when you take it off,' he prophesied.

'If I want any help in taking it off, you can be sure I shan't ask you for it,' Tay flashed. 'When I heard you knock on the door, I thought it was the maid.

'And instead, it was me, bringing you still more flowers.'

With a mocking bow and a flourish. Sven dropped a beribboned cellophane box into her lap.

She looked down at it speechlessly. The delicate spray of tiny orchids was exactly the colour of her hair. She lifted it from its wrapping with fingers that trembled.

'It's beautiful,' she said slowly.

That would have to serve as her thanks. Under any other circumstances, she would have rejoiced in the beauty of the orchids. Coming from Sven, she did not want them.

She flinched away from Sven's touch as he took the corsage from her hands to pin it on to her dress.

'It would look much better on my sash. More unusual.' She stopped him quickly, and took the slender spray back from him and pinned it on to the sash herself.

The effect was stunning. When she entered the reception on Sven's arm a few minutes later, it attracted admiring comment from all sides, and a scowl from Olive, who wore her own orchid—a large and ostentatious one—on her shoulder in the approved manner.

Had Sven given Olive her orchid, too? Tay wondered. And if so, what on earth was Lance doing to allow it? She was left no time for conjecture.

The crews of the competing cars were seated at the top table, another score against her in Olive's eyes, Tay thought, uncaring, and took her seat beside Sven amid a babble of talk and laughter as the crews recounted their various experiences along the Trials route.

Afterwards, Tay could not remember what she ate. She felt too strung up to enjoy the food, and prayed only for the evening to end, so that she could escape back to the privacy of her room and away from Sven, and the increasingly disturbing sensations he fanned into flame inside her.

Even in her room, she would not be able to escape him completely while his flowers still bloomed to remind her of their giver.

The meal dragged to an end, and the gathering electrified with excitement as the speaker rose. His opening speech was mercifully brief, and he came quickly to the eagerly awaited announcements of the results of the Trials.

'The third prize goes to a private entry.' The speaker consulted his notes. 'Douglas and Gordon Weir, from Australia,' he called.

Everyone applauded enthusiastically as the two brothers went up to the rostrum to receive their well earned trophy.

It was a relief to clap, Tay found, to expend her pent-up feelings in a burst of noise and energy. In order to drown her unwelcome thoughts, she clapped as loudly as anyone.

The second prize went to a Norwegian crew, and their presentation over, the speaker paused portentously, deriving the maximum effect from the tense anticipation round the tables.

Tay's attention began to stray. A minute money-spider was crawling over Sven's sleeve, its tiny legs struggling to pull it up over the steep slope of his arm. It had drawn a single strand of web behind it like a lifeline. Tay's eyes followed the slender, silken thread to where it was attached to an outer petal of the topmost orchid on her spray. Like a silver, fairy rope, binding herself and Sven together.

A pang of pain shafted through her. There was no magic in the link for her, only a spell of deception, deliberately woven round her to draw her into the spider's web. Scott's web.

And Sven had willingly allowed himself to become the lure.

The speaker's voice droned on. A thunderous burst of applause erupted round her, and automatically Tay, too, started to clap.

'It's us,' Sven hissed in her ear. 'We've won—you're clapping yourself! Come on.'

He pulled her to her feet, and the movement snapped the slender spider's web.

Tay did not see where its tiny owner went. She walked beside Sven in a daze. His arm was round her waist, propelling her forward. The dinner guests clapped and cheered, and someone took her hand and shook it heartily, uttering words of congratulation.

Sven, as the driver of the camper, was handed the cup. It was large, ornate, and made of solid silver. Under the bright lights, it winked solemnly at Tay from Sven's arms, like a signal across far waters. Tay stared back at it detachedly—the coveted Trials trophy, that would bring herself and Sven international acclaim and the world-wide publicity that would accompany it, and which was so important to both their firms.

And amid the general applause and congratulations that were being showered on them from all sides, something hidden and secret, buried deep in the region of Tay's heart, mourned because a spider's frail web had snapped.

They returned to their place at the table, and a waiter poured champagne into the silver cup, and amid popping of flash bulbs from the press cameras, Sven held the huge goblet to Tay's lips.

'Congratulations, partner,' he smiled.

The intimate acceptance was Tay's undoing. Tears rushed to her eyes and she choked on her mouthful of champagne. Sven held up the cup again, and urged her, 'Have another drink, to clear the way.'

She gulped hurriedly, and the effervescent wine restored her breathing, and boosted her spirits, giving her the strength to laugh up at Sven and repeat gaily, 'Congratulations, partner,' as he, too, quaffed the nectar of victory after her, which all of a sudden tasted of vinegar to Tay.

As victors they were lionised, but they had their duties too, the main one of which was to open the ball.

Guests lined either side of the room, and all eyes were upon them. The orchestra struck up a waltz, but softly, allowing the notes of a solo violin to rise above the other instruments, piercingly sweet, and beckoning Tay and Sven to lead the dance together.

Sven's blue eyes smiled down at her. His arms invited. As if in a dream, Tay drifted into them, and glided away on a cloud of unreality that at any minute might burst and let her down.

But for the moment it cushioned her, soft and sunlit, with only the bright shining edges visible, and the dark, looming centre hidden from her sight, because she resolutely refused to look at it.

One night did not seem much to ask, she thought, grasping at the gilded moments. One night, free from the cut and thrust of company politics on which dubious altar she had been chosen to be the unwilling sacrifice.

One night, when she could dance in Sven's arms without a care, with no thought for the yesterdays, or any care for the tomorrows that, she thought with a quick stab of dread, would bring cares enough of their own.

'Are you enjoying yourself, Copper?' Sven smiled down at her, breaking into her reverie as they circled the ballroom, and she smiled up brightly into his face and replied with brittle conviction, 'Mmm, I'm having a lovely time.'

And if the glitter of the ball, for her, was only the insubstantial tinsel of the champagne she had drunk, who cared—for one night?

Others danced with her, besides Sven. Everyone, it seemed, wanted to dance with the only girl competitor in the Trials—the bearded young giant who had helped her with the stove, other crewmen, whom she recognised, but could not name. She lost count of the number who demanded a dance with her.

And lost sight of Sven.

He caught up with her during an 'excuse-me' dance, and insisted,

'Come back to our own party for a while, and have a break and some supper. They're complaining they haven't seen you all the evening.'

Tay did not want to go back to their own party. She was floating on a high of blissful unreality, and if she went back with Sven to join Scott, and Lance, and Andrew Gleeson—and worst of all, Olive—they would tear her shining cloud apart and bring her tumbling back to earth again.

But she could not ignore her father. She sat down beside Morgan Hilliard and ate the ice-cream Sven brought to her, and tried to make believe the others were not there, but Lance intruded.

'What does it feel like to be belle of the ball?' he teased, with clumsy lack of tact in front of Olive.

'A once-in-a-lifetime experience, I expect,' Olive butted in cattily, and her black eyes hated Tay for her success, envying the attention it brought to her.

'I'm back on earth with a vengeance,' thought Tay, spooning up the last of her ice-cream.

It settled in a cold lump inside her, banishing the warmth of the wine. Beside her, she heard her father and Sven talking. Sven asked quietly,

'Have you heard from Jorgssen yet?' and her father answered, 'Not yet. Give him time.'

Jorgssen? The name struck a chord in Tay's memory. She had heard it mentioned somewhere, quite recently, but she could not remember where. She shrugged, dismissing the tease.

It was a common enough name in its country of origin. It was probably the client her father had been to see in Mombasa. She would ask him later, she decided, when they had a few minutes alone together, and could talk privately.

Suddenly, it seemed to be too much of an effort even to do that. The hectic pace of the last few days, and two hours with not one missed dance, caught up with her, and her head began to spin. She passed a hand wearily across her eyes.

'Have you got a headache, love?' her father asked, with quick concern.

'No, I'm a bit tired, that's all. It's hot in here.'

'Come and take a turn by the pool,' Sven suggested, and reaching down he raised her from her seat. 'It'll be cool by the water.' With a polite, 'Excuse me,' he stepped past Olive, and drew Tay outside, and along the dark, tiled side of the swimming-pool.

It was cooler than she expected. After the heat of the ballroom, and the vigorous exercise of dancing, the air struck chill on her bare arms and shoulders, and she shivered.

'Are you cold?' Sven frowned. 'Don't risk catching a chill. The temperature drops quite sharply out of doors here at night, and you've got nothing on your shoulders.'

'I don't want to go back inside just yet,' Tay objected. 'It's stuffy in the ballroom.'

It was riskier to remain outside, but the risk came from being with Sven, and not from the evening chill. The cold had cleared her head, but the dizzy feeling seemed to have taken possession of her racing pulse instead.

'I'll go and get my wrap,' she said hurriedly.

'I'll fetch it for you,' offered Sven. 'I noticed you left it on your chair. I shan't be a minute. Wait for me, Copper,' he said, and leaning down, he dropped a light kiss on the tip of her nose, before striding away back towards the ballroom on his errand.

Each freckle seemed to tingle at the touch of his lips, and Tay raised her fingers to them, and felt their tips tremble as they touched the place where his lips had rested.

Turning her back hurriedly on the light from the ballroom, she made her way along the side of the swimming-pool, her thoughts in a whirl. Sven was getting under her skin, and she must not allow it to happen. She knew his motives were false, but his constant attentions were beginning to wear away her resistance, like water dripping on a stone. Which was exactly what Sven—and Scott Fielding—intended.

Too late, Tay regretted taking Ken Wallace's place beside Sven in the camper. She should have allowed him to ride the Trials route alone. She doubted if it would have made any difference to the outcome, so far as the Trials results were concerned, and she would not have walked the dangerous tightrope of intimate contact with him for the resulting four days and nights.

Tay regretted allowing Sven to bring her out to the poolside now. She should have excused herself and gone to her room, no matter that she and he would be expected later to lead in the singing of Auld Lang Syne.

Her whole relationship with Sven seemed to be full of regrets, she brooded. If she was not very careful, those regrets might prove to be lasting.

She would not wait for Sven to come back, she decided impulsively. She would go up to her room after all, and come down right at the end of the ball in time to lead the singing with him, and there would be no further opportunity then for them to be alone together.

She half turned, to retrace her steps, and as she did so a footstep sounded behind her. She was too late. 'Sven?' she said, and felt her heart begin to thump again.

There was no answer. Tay caught a whiff of exotic perfume. She felt a hand push her hard in the middle of her back, and the next moment, she was falling, down, down, into the dark, chilled waters of the pool.

She opened her mouth on a startled cry, felt a sharp pain, as her head came into brutal contact with the steel grab-rail that ran along the side of the pool.

She hardly had time to register the cold wetness that reached up to receive her before her mind went blank, and she floated helplessly on her back, her ivory-coloured dress spread like a pale shadow on the silent water.

CHAPTER EIGHT

'TAY! Are you all right? Tay!'

Someone was calling to her.

Someone was kissing her.

Through a haze of slowly returning consciousness, Tay became aware of lips urgent on her own. Her eyelids fluttered open, and the urgency changed, and became something different, something deeper.

'Tay,' muttered Sven hoarsely.

The warmth of his kiss sent a glow through her shivering body, counteracting the cold of her soaking clothes. It parted her bloodless lips, showing the gleam of tiny, even teeth, and she breathed out on a long sigh,

'Sven?'

'Yes, it's me.' His voice sounded curiously rough. 'Thank goodness I saw you! I was going back to look for you in the hotel. I thought you'd got tired of waiting for me, and gone in.' He stopped abruptly. After what seemed a long time he went on, in a more normal voice, 'What happened? You were close to the doors when I left you.'

'Somebody . . .'

The effort to speak was too much for Tay's still swimming head, and she relapsed into silence. She felt Sven's arm tighten round her and lift her gently into a sitting position against him.

With his other hand, he reached behind her, and there was a faint rasp of a ratchet, and, still keeping his arm round her shoulders, he rested her back against some kind of backrest.

She was lying on one of the loungers beside the swimming-pool.

127

The realisation brought her abruptly to full consciousness. Conscious of Sven, cradling her close in his arms, of the fact that he himself was dripping with water, as wet as she was herself.

And of the fact that, even *in extremis*, he had remembered his instructions from his Chairman and carried on kissing her.

A convulsive shudder shook her from head to foot that was not caused by the cold.

'Let me get you into the hotel, before you catch pneumonia,' Sven exclaimed.

He bent to scoop her up into his arms, and Tay recoiled violently from his touch.

'No! I . . . it's better if I walk. I'll get warm that way. Let's run—you're as wet as I am.'

Seconds before her legs had felt like jelly. Now, from somewhere, they found the strength to run. It was a tottering, unsatisfactory sort of run, on feet that seemed to have no feeling in them. But it took her away from Sven.

She hated him with a loathing that frightened her. To kiss her—to carry on his campaign to win her over—while she was still only half conscious . . . He had even fewer scruples than Scott Fielding, who had absolutely none.

She could hear him coming behind her, feel his hands reaching out to support her, and she flogged her legs to still greater efforts to try to outdistance him. A blur of light loomed ahead—the doorway into the hotel. She stumbled through it.

'Tay, love! Whatever's happened?' Her father caught her in his arms. 'Why, you're soaking wet! And there's a bump on your forehead the size of an egg. You're wet, too, Sven.'

'I slipped, and fell into the pool. I didn't see the edge in the darkness,' Tay lied quickly. 'Sven pulled me out. Don't make a fuss, Dad, I'm perfectly all right. I'm just wet, that's all. Let me go and get changed quickly, before anyone sees me in this state. It'll soon be time for Sven and me to lead Auld Lang Syne.'

More than anything else at the moment, she wanted to be on her own. Particularly she wanted to be as far away as possible from Sven.

Cutting short her father's anxious enquiries, and ignoring Sven, she escaped to her room and slipped out of her sopping clothes.

Mercifully she had another dress to change into, the leaf-green and silver one which she had worn to the Federation Dinner. She dropped the ivory silk into the bath with the orchids still attached to the sash. She felt she never wanted to see the dress, or the flowers, again.

So much for Sven's exotic corsage—she gave it a disdainful look, then slammed the bathroom door on it, shutting it from her sight.

Thank goodness her hair was short and naturally curly. She gave it a rub with a towel, flinching as it touched the soreness of her bruised temple. A flick with a comb, and she would be ready to go downstairs again.

She glanced into the mirror, and saw the dark, swelling bruise, like a black flag signalling disaster, on her temple. With a grimace, she reached out and snapped off a white carnation from the nearest vase. One of Sven's carnations, but there was nothing else to hand, and she gripped it into her hair, allowing it to fall softly to one side, and looked at it critically to see the effect.

It made a dainty contrast to her bright curls and effectively hid the swelling, and by the time the bruise had darkened to any noticeable extent the evening would be over. And so as long no one searched her eyes they would not see the pain that lurked deep in their green depths.

Sven had kissed her while she was still only half conscious, and it hurt. He had grasped the opportunity when she was at her most vulnerable to further his

Chairman's vile instructions. Striking while the iron's hot, he would probably call it, she thought bitterly. Well, he had struck. And the blow had left an indelible mark.

It should not have hurt her so much, knowing why he had kissed her. She had known his reasons all along. But the hurt inside her far surpassed the hurt to her bruised head, and bewilderment added to the already confused state of her thoughts.

She did not doubt for a moment that she had been deliberately pushed into the pool, nor whose hand it was that had done the pushing. It could only be Olive's. Her heavy, exotic perfume hung in Tay's nostrils still. But it was pointless to try to accuse her. How could she prove it? Olive would merely shrug in her insolent way, and accuse Tay of trying to make trouble.

Tay sighed, and put aside the problem until later. If she did not go down, Sven might come up to her room to fetch her.

The last waltz was just ending as she entered the ballroom, and Tay breathed a sigh of pure relief. She had escaped having to dance with Sven.

He looked at her searchingly as she joined him, but she avoided meeting his eyes, and the band struck up Auld Lang Syne, which effectively prevented him from asking any questions for the moment.

She could not avoid him taking her by the hand, but she allowed her own to remain limp and unresponsive in his grasp as they joined the swaying line of people on either side of them.

'Should auld acquaintance be forgot ...'

If only she had never become acquainted with Sven! If only she could forget him, now she had.

Tay slipped away the moment the singing was over, and by dint of sticking closely to her father she managed to escape upstairs to her room without being alone with Sven again.

'Have a good lie-in,' Morgan Hilliard advised her the

next morning when he put his head round her bedroom
door first thing to see how she felt.

'I don't need to, I feel fine,' she protested. 'A bang on
the head and a ducking isn't enough to stop me from
joining the trip to the game park today.' Deliberately she
played down the incident of the evening before.

She decided not to mention her suspicions about Olive
to her father. She would have a word with that woman
herself, later, when the opportunity presented itself, she
promised herself grimly. She did not flatter Olive by
describing her as a lady, even in her own thoughts.

'The safari doesn't start until ten o'clock, so you've got
ample time,' Morgan Hilliard insisted. 'Have a quiet
start. Your temple's black and blue this morning. I'll
have your breakfast sent up to your room.'

He disappeared downstairs in search of his own, and
Tay was hesitating whether or not to follow him
notwithstanding, when the advantages of eating in her
own room presented themselves.

By this means she could avoid meeting Sven until it
was time to start out for the game park. It was an
eminently satisfactory arrangement from her point of
view, and she bathed and dressed in a leisurely fashion,
making the most of her temporary reprieve.

Her next problem was how best to disguise the bruise
on her temple. Her own make-up, which she used only on
occasion, was too light to cover up the dark discoloration,
and she shrank from running the gauntlet of comments
and questions, which sight of the bruise was bound to
cause when she went downstairs.

Olive was the only woman who used the heavy,
pancake variety of make-up that would be adequate for
such a purpose, and for obvious reasons she did not want
to ask her for the loan of some.

A white carnation would look out of place on a safari,
and Tay had not got a bush hat. She drew her curls down
experimentally over her temple, but they persisted in

springing back again, and finally she flung down her hairbrush in disgust.

'There's no help for it, I'll have to use Sven's kerchief,' she decided reluctantly.

It held the curls in place so that they covered all but the very edge of the bruise, and she hoped the bright splash of colour in the patterned cotton would distract anyone's eye away from her face and on to the kerchief itself.

She disposed of the difficulty of whether or not to wear Sven's bracelet by leaving her yellow dress in the wardrobe, and wearing fawn cotton slacks and a shirt to match instead, and leaving off all jewellery except her wristwatch.

'You look very workmanlike in that outfit,' Sven approved.

The maid brought in the breakfast tray, and before she could shut the door behind her, Sven followed, so close on the girl's heels that he might have been her shadow. With a smile, she put down the tray and withdrew, and Tay expostulated,

'It's too early for the safari yet. I was told it doesn't start until ten o'clock.'

'No more it doesn't,' he agreed. 'I came to see how your head was this morning.'

With quickened breath, Tay wished he had not bothered. Although she had put a brave front on her ducking the night before, the episode had shaken her more than she cared to admit, and she did not feel ready to cope with Sven just yet, particularly in the intimacy of her bedroom. After breakfast, and in the company of the others, she would feel more confident to face him again, but not now.

To cover her unease, she spoke flippantly.

'Do you mean after the bruise it received, or after the champagne I drank last night?' She saw his jaw tighten, and she added hastily, 'You could have asked Dad. There was no need for you to invade my room.'

'I preferred to come and see for myself.' Sven bent down, and with fingers that were feather-light he eased back the curls and the kerchief, making it plain that it was the bruise, and not the champagne, he was interested in.

He scowled at what he saw, but his face was above Tay's head, and she did not see.

'I took ages getting the kerchief right, and now you've disturbed it,' she grumbled and tugged the cotton square back into place again.

'I seem to have disturbed its owner, as well.' Sven's fingers came up under her chin, and tipped up her face to meet his.

'Why should you disturb me?' she countered, and cursed the rich tide of colour that flooded her throat and cheeks, betraying her confusion.

'My mother always used to kiss our bruises better, when we were little,' Sven remarked. 'I wonder if the magic still works.'

He bent, and dropped the lightest whisper of a kiss on Tay's multi-coloured temple. She flinched away, but not before the brush of lips speeded her pulse with the swift acceleration that she had come to dread.

'The bruise is better,' she began.

'Because I kissed it? So the magic *does* still work.'

'Yes . . . *No!*' Tay contradicted herself, raggedly, and hated the laughter that made his blue eyes dance.

The pulse underneath the bruise jerked into erratic life, making the tender veins of her temple throb. But the throbbing no longer hurt. Could it be because of Sven's kiss? Nervously she jinked away from the reason that it no longer hurt, and emphasised firmly, 'It felt better *before*. If it weren't for the colour, I'd have forgotten all about it by now.'

'Just like you forgot to thank me for rescuing you from the pool last night?' Sven chided her. 'I ruined a perfectly good evening suit, fishing you out of the water.'

'Of all the cheek!' she exploded. 'I don't consider I've got anything to thank you for. It was your fault I was pushed into the pool in the first place.'

'Did you say *pushed*?' Sven latched on to the word immediately, and stared at her with suddenly narrowed eyes.

Tay bit her lip vexedly. She had not meant to say anything about her suspicions. She preferred to deal with Olive herself. But it was out now, and there was nothing she could do to retract it.

'Yes, I said pushed,' she reiterated. 'If you must know, it was Olive who did the pushing.'

'You must be imagining things!'

'I didn't imagine the smell of her perfume the second before I felt a hand give me a hard shove in the back.'

'Anyone can wear perfume,' Sven reminded her. 'But if that's what you think, at least you can't blame me for your ducking.'

'If you hadn't been playing Don Juan with a married woman, it wouldn't have happened!' declared Tay, too incensed to be careful now of what she said.

As soon as the words were out of her mouth, she knew she had gone too far.

Sven's eyes swept over her with a look that brought a gasp of fright to her lips.

'Of all the suspicious, ungrateful little . . .' he growled, and reached towards her.

Tay fought him, but the steel band of his arms held her easily. They clamped round her, curbing her struggles without apparent effort, while his mouth bored into hers, hard, and angry, punishing her for her ingratitude in not thanking him for pulling her out of the pool, punishing her for accusing Olive.

He took his time to exact payment for rescuing her, a long, long time. Tay was panting and furious when he finally let her go.

'I detest you!' she cried, wiping an angry hand over her lips.

'You'd be better occupied in eating your breakfast than in making wild accusations you can't possibly prove,' Sven snapped, and swinging round he picked up the daintily laden tray, and deposited it ungently on to her lap. 'While you're about it, chew on this,' he grated. 'I don't play Don Juan with any woman, least of all with a married one!'

In two strides he was at the door and through it, and he closed it behind him with a thud that boldly underscored his parting shot.

Tay ate her breakfast mechanically. Had Sven told her the truth? Was there, in fact, nothing between himself and Olive? His anger at her accustation was convincing.

So were his kisses, and she knew the real reason behind those, she reminded herself savagely.

Sven should have joined his godfather in Hollywood. As a plausible actor, he would make top of the charts, or whatever, in no time.

Olive's behaviour towards him was blatant and inexcusable for a married woman, and she would not persist if she did not receive encouragement.

One part of Tay weakly longed to believe Sven, while common sense argued that it would be madness to do so when his whole attitude to herself was a living lie.

It was almost ten o'clock. Time to go. She reached for her bag, ready filled with all the necessities for the day, and slung it over her shoulder. Her eager anticipation in the coming safari was gone. In its place, a black dread gripped her at the prospect of spending yet another day wth the Fielding ménage, at the mercy of their unscrupulous machinations.

The safari vehicle proved to be air-conditioned and roomy, with sufficient space in it for their small party to have a window-seat each, which promised spectacular viewing.

Olive grabbed the front single seat, next to the driver,
which gave her a wide front view, as well as the one to her
side.

It must mean that Sven would be driving, Tay
deduced, and she quietly went to the rear of the vehicle.

Lance sat in the first double seat, behind Olive, and
invited his wife to 'Come and sit by me,' and scowled
when she answered with a shrug, 'No, I want to sit here. I
can see more.'

See more of Sven, she meant, Tay surmised. She had
scant sympathy for Lance. She despised him for not
taking sterner measures with Olive. He must be blind not
to have noticed his wife's advances to Sven, and spineless
to do nothing about them.

The hotel had provided them with a large hamper of
food which lay on the seat on the opposite side of the
gangway to Tay, which would ensure that no one sat
there, she saw with satisfaction.

Her father, Scott and Andrew Gleeson distributed
themselves about the vehicle, and to make sure that no
one tried to occupy the space beside herself, Tay took the
precaution of placing her shoulder bag, binoculars and
camera ostentatiously spread right across it.

This was better than she had anticipated, and her
spirits began to rise.

Sven confirmed her prediction by slipping into the
driving-seat opposite to Olive, but Olive had no
opportunity for private conversation with him if that had
been her aim.

As soon as he set the vehicle in motion, Sven spoke
through a microphone set on the dashboard in front of
him.

'I know the game reserve well,' he told them. 'I'll point
out any animals which you might not be quick to spot for
yourselves, and warn you of any that are coming up in
front of us, so that you can watch out for them as we pass
by.'

He drove slowly, and there followed three of the most enthralling hours Tay had ever experienced. She forgot everything except the constant procession of wild-life that passed in front of her wondering eyes.

'There's a giraffe, feeding on the acacia trees to your right,' Sven called. 'If you look very closely, you'll see her young one deeper into the shadows of the thicket.'

The mottled camouflage was so effective, their unaccustomed eyes would surely have missed the young one otherwise.

'There's a family of lions coming up in front,' he announced, and slowed the vehicle so that Tay could photograph them, then,

'Watch that patch of scrub, on your right. A cheetah with her cubs is lying up in the shade.'

Tay's eyes were kept constantly swivelling from one side of the bus to the other, so as not to miss a single moment of the wonder of this huge, wild Noah's ark, that never in her wildest dreams had she imagined could be half so wonderful as this.

'Sing out when you want to stop for photographs,' called Sven.

'I must have one of those hippos!' Tay exclaimed. Then, 'Oh, he's disappeared!' she cried, disappointed, as her subject submerged disobligingly in the muddy waters of a sluggish river.

'Take him now, quickly,' urged Sven, as the huge amphibian surfaced again seconds later, and Tay clicked happily, and begged, 'Now, one of those buffalo.'

'They're a bit too close for comfort,' Sven objected, and kept the vehicle rolling.

He was just being awkward, she decided crossly. 'They look quiet enough,' she protested as the buffalo raised their heads and gazed towards the vehicle with sad eyes from under their huge, curved horns, and looked as if they would not hurt a fly.

'Buffalo can be unpredictable,' Sven retorted, unmoved by her plea. 'There'll be more, at a safer distance, later on.'

There were lots more, and Tay used up film with reckless abandon.

'Surely you've taken enough photographs by now?' complained Olive, becoming bored, and showing it.

'I can't ever have enough of this,' Tay enthused, and raised her camera yet again to point it at a group of maribou storks.

Olive's click of annoyance drowned the shutter as Sven patiently halted the vehicle until Tay had taken her snap, and she muttered an audible, 'Thank goodness for that,' when he said firmly, 'One more, and then we must stop for lunch.'

'It can't be as late as that!'

But it was, and soon they rolled to a halt amid an attractive group of tourist lodges dotted about among a stand of trees, and decanted from the mini-bus, not without some relief, to stretch their legs.

'It's stupid, making us stay cooped inside a vehicle all the time,' Olive grumbled. 'We could just as well have got out to look at the animals.'

'It's a Park rule that no one's allowed to leave their vehicle. It's designed for your own safety,' Sven told her. 'This isn't a zoo, you know. The animals are truly wild, and we're encroaching on their territory. They don't take any notice of a vehicle, as a rule, but a human being on foot would be a different matter altogether. It's best not to risk a confrontation, and possible tragedy.'

'I still think it's stupid, just the same,' snapped Olive, and when Lance indicated one of the small lodges, and told her 'That one's been reserved for the ladies, if you'd like to freshen up before lunch,' she stamped up the step and into the miniature bungalow without having the grace to say, 'Thank you.'

Tay followed her slowly.

She would have preferred to wait until Olive was

finished, but she guessed the other girl would deliberately keep her waiting for as long as possible, which would mean unduly delaying lunch for them. So with a shrug she made the best of it, and followed Olive into the shady interior.

Olive had already taken possession of the only available wash-basin, and Tay was conscious of her black eyes in the mirror above it, challenging her to try to share it, but Olive neither spoke nor turned round as Tay entered, so she availed herself of the shower for her own wash.

She was obliged to use the mirror above the wash-basin to comb her hair. Spitefully, Olive moved to block as much of it as she could, but it was long enough for two, and Tay pulled off the kerchief and ran her comb through her short curls. Freed from their restriction, they sprang back from her forehead, and revealed the bruise on her temple.

Olive's eyes fixed on to it immediately.

'The next time you walk by a swimming-pool, make sure you haven't had too much to drink,' she sneered.

'It wasn't the champagne that overbalanced me, and you know it!' Tay was stung to retort.

'*I* know it? What do you mean?' cried Olive.

'What I said,' Tay returned bluntly, and her eyes met Olive's like chips of green ice through the mirror. 'The next time you decide to push someone into the pool, make sure you're not wearing that ghastly heavy perfume you like so much,' she suggested coldly. 'It's a dead giveaway.'

'You're out of your mind,' Olive shrilled, but Tay thought she detected a flicker of fear in the glittering black eyes. 'When you cracked your head on the grab-rail of the pool, it must have knocked all the sense out of you!'

'How did you know what I hit my head on? I didn't even know myself.'

'I . . . I . . .' Olive's face went livid, and Tay almost felt sorry for her.

She eyed her stonily, 'You're not worth bothering with,' she told her in a voice loaded with contempt. 'Just don't try anything like it again, that's all. I might not feel so inclined to let you get away with it a second time.'

'Are you girls going to stay in there gossiping all day?' Sven's voice shouted in at the doorway. 'If you don't hurry, we'll eat your share of the lunch!'

'Coming!' Tay called back, and without deigning to give Olive another glance, she quickly replaced the kerchief, and swinging on her heel she marched outside to join Sven, determinedly pushing Olive's unpleasantness to the back of her mind.

The lunch was laid out in buffet form on a table on the veranda of the next lodge, with chairs scattered in the tree-shaded, paved area in front of it.

There was a multitude of dainties, designed to satisfy the hearty appetites of travellers, and Sven helped Tay to load her plate, then sat down beside her underneath the trees.

Olive sat glowering at them from a distance, but she could hardly do otherwise than sit by Lance, and made her discontent obvious by her constant complaints about the food and the drink, and the discomfort of her chair.

Her voice faded into the background as Sven said quietly. 'You enjoyed this morning, didn't you, Copper.' It was a statement rather than a question, and his voice held a quiet satisfaction that his planned outing had been such a success.

'It's been perfect,' said Tay, and her glowing face was ample proof, if any were needed, of just how much she had enjoyed the morning.

Whatever Sven had done to her, at least he had given her this, and she hugged it to her as the one—and only—good memory she would have to carry away with her in connection with him.

'It's an absolute Garden of Eden!' she enthused.

'And Eve's reluctant to leave it?'

'It would be lovely to stay on for a while,' Tay admitted. 'I've always wanted to visit the game-reserves, ever since I was small. I've been abroad, of course, but never this far before. And now . . .'

She broke off. Now, there would be no money to spend on such luxuries, unless they either merged with Fieldings, or some miracle occurred to put Hilliard Engineering on to its financial feet again.

Quickly, Tay shied away from the reminder. It must not be allowed to mar the day, but she could not help admitting wistfully, 'It would be wonderful to have a really long holiday here, with time to view the game properly.'

'Maybe you'll be able to do that soon. Life holds a lot of surprises,' Sven observed, contentedly making inroads into his own plateful of food.

Bleakly, Tay doubted it. The surprises life had held in store for her recently had all been of the unpleasant kind, and Sven himself numbered among them. Life would never be the same, for her, after meeting him, she realised suddenly, and she still had that knowledge to come to terms with.

She finished her pineapple dessert and stood up.

'I'm going to see if there's anything come to the water-hole,' she said, and grabbing her camera, she jumped to her feet, goaded into activity by the unwelcome thought.

'Don't stray away from the viewing area,' Sven warned her.

'I wouldn't be so silly,' she assured him, and hurried away.

It was worse than silly to allow herself to be so affected by Sven. He was beginning to dominate her thoughts as well as her actions.

Restlessly, she wandered to the edge of the veranda above the water-hole. It was screened from view of the

chairs set beneath the trees, and with a sigh she leaned on
the rail and looked down, glad to fix her weary mind on a
life other than her own.

There were a number of animals come to drink. A
family of wild pigs squealed and squabbled among
themselves. They looked vicious. Tay noticed the other
creatures, even the larger animals, gave them a wide
berth.

A couple of zebras trotted down to the edge of the pool
to drink, and a giraffe splay-legged to allow its muzzle to
reach the water. Tay wished she had invested in a ciné
camera instead of one that took only stills.

A soft step sounded immediately behind her, and she
whirled round, her hand gripping convulsively on to the
rail of the viewing veranda, and feeling the colour drain
from her face.

'Sorry if I scared you,' said Sven, and his eyes
narrowed, searching her face.

'You startled me, that's all.' Tay recovered herself
quickly. 'I didn't know it was you,' she said lamely.

She had thought for an unnerved moment that it might
be Olive, bent on further mischief after their quarrel in
the lodge. Her experience at the pool had left her edgy,
and she did not fancy being pitchforked into the middle
of the herd of wild pigs, which Sven had mentioned
during the morning would attack at the least provoca-
tion.

She turned her face away from him to look over the
veranda rail again, using the animals as an excuse to hide
her expression from him.

'Tay——' he began, and his hand reached out to grip
her by the arm and turn her back to face him again.

'Is there anything worth looking at?' Lance enquired,
strolling to join them. To Tay's relief, Olive was not with
him.

'There's some wild pigs—come and look! And a lovely
giraffe, and ...' Hurriedly Tay drew Lance to the rail

beside her, aware of his amused glance towards Sven at her eager enthusiasm.

She was overdoing it, but it could not be helped. Lance would serve as a barrier to keep Sven at bay, and with Olive's husband between them, there was no chance of his trying to start a private conversation.

Did he guess the reason for her fright when he came soft-footed behind her? The answer was beside the point, since Tay was in no mood to be cross-questioned on the subject, particularly as Sven had practically accused her of lying, when she told him Olive had pushed her into the pool.

She had no intention of discussing the matter with him any further. She had said what she had to say to Olive personally, and that was that, and she determined to enjoy the rest of the safari free from the loaded atmosphere that had dogged her every hour in Kenya so far.

'Tell me, do the wild pigs always go round in family groups like that?' She pestered the men with questions, asking another almost before she got an answer to the one before.

By dint of pretending to be a complete ignoramus on the habits of the wild, which her well thumbed volumes on the subject that crammed her bookshelves at home would have told her willing informants was by no means the case, Tay managed to keep Lance beside her, and Sven at bay, until it was time to return to the mini-bus and resume the safari.

Lance took the wheel on the return journey, which left Sven free to choose his own seat where he willed. To Tay's surprise, he bypassed the seat directly behind Olive, and quickly Tay slid into the space beside her father, foiling any possibility of Sven coming to sit with her.

Undeterred by her obvious snub, he commandeered the seat in front of them and occupied himself by pointing out to them the most interesting sights passing by their window.

'You're very knowledgeable on the subject,' Morgan Hilliard remarked appreciatively, as Sven identified individuals among a mixed flock of birds feeding in the grasses.

'I became friends with one of the wardens on the game reserve when I was living out here. I spent most of my off-duty time with him, and he passed on a lot of his knowledge to me. And all his enthusiasm,' Sven smiled.

Lucky Sven.

Luckless Tay, she thought bleakly, that her own once-in-a-lifetime experience of the game reserve should be in such fraught company.

Black cones began to appear on the surface of the plain. 'They're volcanic,' Sven explained. 'Some of them are extinct, but according to what a Trials marshal told me, there have been eruptions from the others fairly recently. The threat's always there, of course, lying just underneath the surface.'

Her own emotions seemed to be in much the same state, Tay brooded. She felt as if a veritable cauldron bubbled under the surface of her mind, that, if it should erupt, would destroy her utterly.

The threatening black cones suddenly depressed her, and peversely she was glad when at length they left the game reserve behind them, and regained the bright bustle of Nairobi's busy streets.

As soon as they got back to the hotel Sven immediately left Tay and her father to make their own way inside together, and he ran up the hotel steps to catch up with Olive, as if he had done his duty by squiring Tay for the moment, and could not wait to pursue his own more interesting occupations.

Tay watched him take Olive's arm and walk her up the hotel steps, and on the way he paused and spoke to

Lance, but his tone was low, and she could not hear what he said.

The other man looked startled, Tay thought, and then all three disappeared inside the hotel together, and Tay did not see them again until an hour later, after she had bathed away the dust of the day, and was dressing ready to go downstairs to dinner.

Her bedroom window was wide open, and Lance's voice floated through it from the tarmac below.

It was hard, and angry. 'You're coming with me, whether you like it or not,' it said sternly to someone, in a tone that Tay had never heard Lance use before.

Curiosity drew her to the window. The mini-bus was still parked on the forecourt, and Olive was beside it, with Lance holding firmly on to her arm. Her eyes looked red, as if she had been crying.

Tay stared down at them, startled, and Sven appeared in her range of vision.

'Shall I drive you?' he offered to Lance.

'No, thanks, Sven—I'll drive. I'll deal with this madam myself,' Lance said, and Tay's eyebrows rose.

The worm had turned.

Tay did not like Lance, but she disliked him less than all the others of the Fielding Board, and she was glad to see him in control of his wife for once.

Evidently he had had a row with Olive and Sven about their affair together, and had decided—not before it was time—to put an end to it.

As Tay watched, Lance thrust his wife ungently into the mini-bus, and with a nod in Sven's direction, he got in himself and drove off, and Sven walked back into the hotel, and out of Tay's sight.

'It serves him right,' she muttered, as she finished dressing. And wondered, with a malicious pleasure that left her feeling shocked at her own unaccustomed spite, exactly how Sven would explain Olive's absence at dinner.

CHAPTER NINE

TAY'S curiosity had to remain unappeased.

Sven did not put in an appearance at dinner, and neither, to her surprise, did Scott, or Andrew Gleeson.

'Where is everybody?' Tay asked her father, and Morgan Hilliard replied,

'They're having a meeting and a working dinner in Scott's suite.'

'Do they begrudge the few hours they spend on an outing so much that they have to make up the time by working in the evening?'

'I imagine something important's cropped up. It was Sven who called the meeting. He looked very put out about something, I thought.'

He would be, Tay thought. Olive was gone. Out loud she said bluntly,

'They won't be missed. You and I can have our meal in peace for once. We haven't had a chance to talk together since I came back from the Trials run.'

'No, and I've got lots to tell you,' Morgan Hilliard said.

Tay smiled. It was good to see her father so enthusiastic again. The day on the game reserve had evidently done him good. It certainly seemed to have removed the cloud of worry from his face that had rested there for far too long.

'Talk away,' she encouraged. 'Have you had many enquiries for our engine?'

'Dozens,' her father gloated. 'And I've got several firm orders, too. The very moment we get home, I'll have to . . .'

'Do you mind if we join you?' A couple from one of the Trials teams strolled across to their table, and Tay groaned inwardly. Much as she liked them both, she urgently wanted to talk with her father on their own. The enquiries he had received, and better still the orders, made splendid news. But it also made a merger with Fieldings that much more inevitable.

People who ordered engines would not expect to wait for ever for them to be delivered, and unless they could expand their capacity quickly enough to cope, the customers would lose interest and go elsewhere for their needs.

And from where, apart from Scott Fielding, could they raise the necessary capital?

Tay felt as if the jaws of a trap were inexorably closing round her. She hardly heard the conversation going on round her. The two men seemed content to go on talking for the rest of the evening.

'It's a pity Sven isn't here,' Morgan Hillard remarked hospitably.

'Yes, isn't it?' the two echoed, but from the looks which each continued to cast in Tay's direction, they were more than happy to continue with the company as it stood, and remained firmly glued to Tay and her father for the rest of the evening until at last, pleading weariness, she gave up all hope of a private talk with Morgan Hilliard for the moment, and escaped to her room.

Her father was due to start back for Mombasa immediately after breakfast the next morning, and Tay bided her time until then with what patience she could muster.

She would go with him to the coast, she decided. In the car together they would have the opportunity to talk without being interrupted, and at the same time it would have the dual advantage of removing her out of the orbit of Sven and his co-directors.

Without Olive to distract him for part of the time, Tay did not trust herself to be able to withstand the added pressure Sven would be able to put upon her during the time when her father would be absent.

Sven himself blocked her plan as soon as he joined them at breakfast.

The meal had been arranged especially early for Morgan Hilliard's benefit, and Tay was surprised when Sven walked into the room. Fortunately it was still much too early for Scott or Andrew Gleeson to put in an appearance as well.

Sven has probably been awake all night, fretting over Olive, Tay told herself, but one look at his fresh, alert face and bright eyes gave the lie to her assumption. He looked as if he had nothing on his mind—or his conscience—beyond the pleasant anticipation of an interesting day's business ahead.

He sat down with them, and shook out his napkin, and enquired politely of Morgan Hilliard, 'Is it all right if I borrow Tay today?'

As if she was some kind of possession, to be loaned and returned at will, with no say whatever in the matter herself!

'I've had an interesting enquiry from someone in Malindi,' Sven went on, without deigning so much as to glance in Tay's direction. 'They run excursions for tourists, and they think a modified version of our larger camper might suit their needs.'

'Why drag me along?' Tay protested, seeing her plans to accompany her father beginning to fade into the distance. 'Surely you don't need my help to sell your own company's products?'

'They want an expert run-down on the engine,' Sven explained, 'And since your father will be in Mombasa all day . . .'

'There's Ken Wallace.'

'Ken's having his plaster eased at the hospital today. The heat's making it uncomfortable. You're the only one left who's got a detailed knowledge of the engine,' Sven

replied, and made Tay feel as if he was taking her along
with him only as a last resort.

'Go ahead,' Morgan Hilliard readily gave his permission, and Tay gritted her teeth helplessly. 'I'll have to stay
overnight in Mombasa myself.'

'That'll make it easier all round,' Sven remarked.
'We'll have to stay overnight in Malindi. There won't be
time to come all the way back to Nairobi after the
meeting. Our client wants a trial run, as well as detailed
discussions. Scott's following us down later, to meet
someone else there, so we can all fly back home from
Mombasa. Andrew flies home this morning, so he won't
be coming with us.'

'What about Lance and Olive?' asked Tay, unable to
help herself.

She was not sure what reaction she expected from
Sven, but whatever it was she was due to be disappointed.

His face remained smoothly impassive, and his casual
tone hid whatever it was he might be feeling on the
subject. 'Oh, they flew out last night. Didn't you know?'

'I didn't receive the circular telling me about it,' Tay's
voice bit.

Olive had been taken home in disgrace. In that case,
Sven should have gone too. Tay silently condemned him
for leaving Olive to shoulder all the blame.

It was weak and cowardly, and despising him as she
did, this further evidence of Sven's unprincipled behaviour should not have made her feel so miserable. Tay
pushed aside her breakfast with sudden lack of appetite,
and concentrated on her coffee, not looking at Sven.

'I'll leave you two to finish your meal.' Morgan
Hilliard rose, and dropped a light kiss on Tay's forehead.
'I've got a couple of telephone calls to make before I set
off.'

Which meant he did not want to be disturbed, she
deduced. Their talk would have to wait now until they

met tomorrow in Mombasa. Suddenly, tomorrow seemed
a hundred years away.

'Take good care of her,' her father bade Sven, only half
jokingly. 'Make sure she doesn't collect any more bumps.
This bruise clashes with the colour of her curls!'

'There's no danger of a repeat performance,' Sven
answered, with such conviction that Tay's eyes flew up to
search his face. Had he come round to believing what she
told him after all? Did he know that, now Olive was
gone, she was in no danger of another ducking? Or was
he just saying it to make conversation?

Sven's expression told her nothing, as he added, 'I'll
take care of her, Morgan, never fear.'

In his own interests, he probably would not let her out
of his sight.

Tay gave him a stony look when he turned to her and
said, 'How long will it take you to pack your case,
Copper?'

'It's already packed,' Tay returned shortly. 'I'd
planned to go with Dad to Mombasa.'

She made no attempt to hide her disappointment at the
unexpected turn of events, but since she could not reverse
them, there was no point in trying to delay their
departure from the hotel.

She felt as if she were taking part in the last stages of a
drama that was poised to reach its climax just before the
curtain dropped.

It was a relief that Olive and Lance, and now Andrew
Gleeson, had left the stage, but Tay wondered uneasily
how many of the enquiries her father would be dealing
with in Mombasa had been engineered by Scott Fielding
in order to remove him safely out of the way as well.

Sven and Scott between them had manipulated things
very effectively to get Tay on her own before they all flew
back home, and during the coming two days they would
be at liberty between them to exert as much pressure on

her as they pleased in order to bring her round to their
way of thinking.

'I mustn't crack,' she warned herself. If she did, it
would swing the balance of opinion on the merger in
Scott's favour.

Morgan Hilliard respected Tay's opinion, and during
the last year or two he had come to rely on her in the
business, as he would have done had she been a son, and
was wont to treat her almost as an equal partner.

Armed with a pocketful of new orders, and the need to
expand quickly to meet them, Tay's defection would be
sufficient to swing her father over to agreeing to the
merger, and thus handing over his own life's work to
Scott Fielding.

If only there were another way ...

Her father's car started off from the forecourt as she
left the dining-room. The two telephone calls must have
been brief. Tay walked slowly upstairs, frowning
thoughtfully. Sven was walking out through the lobby
when she returned with her luggage. A car was parked
outside, and one of the reporters covering the Trials
walked beside Sven with his case in his hand. He was
questioning Sven.

'Is it true, Mr Diamond, that Fieldings are about to
merge with Hilliard Engineering? I've heard a rumour
flying round.'

'That's all it is. Just a rumour.' Sven spoke easily. 'You
know how these things start. We're using the Hilliard
engine in our new camper because it's far and away the
best power-unit on the market today.'

'Thanks very much,' muttered Tay under her breath.

'You can take my word for it,' Sven went on to the
attentively listening reporter, 'there's no truth in what
you've heard. Our relationship with Hilliard's is merely
that of an ordinary customer. Can we give you a lift to the
airport?' He changed the subject as if it held no interest
for him, and Tay stared astounded at his retreating back.

What deviousness was he plotting now? Surely Scott had not changed his mind about wanting a merger at this stage?

In the motoring press the engine had received even more enthusiastic publicity than the camper itself, which had accolades enough bestowed on it as a result of the Trials victory.

On top of this, there was the stream of enquiries which Morgan Hilliard had received from would-be customers for the engine.

Surely that should make Scott Fielding all the keener to link their two companies together? So why the sudden volte-face?

Were the enquiries genuine? Tay worried. Or were they merely red herrings, carefully laid by Scott or Sven, to entice her father to put every last penny he owned into remaining independent of Fieldings, and expanding on his own? And then, when the enquiries proved to be groundless, and the orders for the engines were not forthcoming, her father would be faced with bankruptcy and be forced to let his company go for a mere pittance.

To Scott Fielding, of course.

It was unscrupulous, and without mercy, and typical of Scott and his Board. It was also legitimate business tactics, Tay realised, dry-mouthed. Such things had been done before, and doubtless would be done again. But for Sven to stand by and see it being done to her father, and actually taking a leading role in it himself . . .

She marched out to the car with a seething rage in her heart against Sven that made the volcanic cones on the plains of yesterday look like a mere kettle boiling over.

During the short car journey to the airport, the presence of the reporter was a welcome distraction, and as soon as they boarded the plane, Sven opened his briefcase, and began to study a clipboard of typed notes. After a few minutes, he passed the top one to Tay to look at.

'Samuel Linkman is the client we're going to see,' he said, and smiled. 'Nice name for a tour operator, don't you think? He caters for the luxury end of the market. He was impressed by the high specification of the Hilliard engine, and the go-anywhere aspect of the camper itself, combined with a standard of comfort not usually associated with such a vehicle. By the end of today, with a bit of luck, we'll have brought off a good order between us, and added another customer to our books.'

His brisk anticipation held all the excitement of the chase, and in spite of herself, the thrill communicated itself to Tay. She was sharing the chase with him, just as she had in the Trials.

And then she remembered, and the thrill died, and black depression took its place. Every bit of help she gave Sven was like hammering a nail into the coffin of Hilliard Engineering.

The flight to Mombasa was comparatively brief, and in a fraction of the time it would have taken them by road they were touching down on the runway, and Sven was taking possession of a large sleek car that was standing waiting for them.

'The agents arranged for it to be here,' he said, accepting the service as a matter of course, and Tay observed critically,

'I notice you don't travel in your own products.'

'The camper was sent on ahead of us by road, last night, to save time. When we get there, Mr Linkman and his staff will have got through any trial runs they want to make and be ready to talk business.'

'Do you drive one of the Fieldings range yourself, when you're at home?' she asked, in the polite, impersonal voice she would have used to any acquaintance, and Sven threw her an oblique look before he answered.

'Fieldings only make leisure vehicles. They're not

suitable for everyday business use. As a matter of fact, I own a Hilliard myself.'

'A Hilliard?' echoed Tay. 'I didn't know you were a customer of ours.

'Mine's a vintage model. It would be a bit before your time.'

'Does Dad know? He might like to see your car, to check how it's weathered,' she exclaimed. In the face of Sven's surprising revelation, she forgot her antagonism for the moment.

'I mentioned it to him,' Sven replied. 'I've told him he can have a look at it any time he wants to. But we've both been so busy since then, we haven't had time to settle on a date. It won't be for a while anyway. My godfather's borrowed it for the next few months.'

'The film director? Then it must be in the States.'

Tay let the matter of the car drop. By the time Sven had it back in his own garage she hoped that by some miracle Hilliard's financial problems would be solved, and their connection with Fieldings—and Sven—nothing more than a bad dream. It was a forlorn hope, but it was all she had.

'Now you know I'm a customer of your firm, you'll have to be especially nice to me,' teased Sven, and Tay felt an urge to smack him.

'You don't miss a trick, do you?' she retorted, and added, 'what are you stopping for?'

The car pulled to the side of the road, and Sven braked it to a halt overlooking a vision of pale sand, and blue, sparkling ocean, and waving palm trees.

'We're much too early for our appointment with Mr Linkman,' Sven flashed a quick glance at his wristwatch. 'We might as well sit here, and enjoy the view while we can.'

His eyes rested on Tay's face, not on the view.

He reached down, and in a leisurely fashion pressed the seat-belt locks, and the straps snaked away, leaving them both free. Tay shifted nervously in her seat.

'Relax,' Sven smiled, and promptly made taking his advice impossible by reaching out and drawing her to him.

'Don't! We're on a public road,' Tay protested, grasping at the first excuse that came into her head. She raised urgent hands to push herself away from him. Her heart hammered. With dilating eyes, she strained away from Sven's hold. Her pulses raced, and if she allowed him to kiss her, it would be all that was needed to push her overcharged emotion irredeemably over the lip of a precipice which she had, until now, tried to make herself believe did not exist. What a fool she had been, not to have seen the danger before. She had to stop him quickly, before it was too late.

'Don't!' she pleaded, and to her horror she felt her eyes suffuse with tears.

'Why not?' he countered. His lips brushed her own, moving tantalisingly across her mouth. 'I'm a valued customer of Hilliards.'

'I don't play games with customers.' Tay tried ineffectually to pull away from him.

His lips teased her mouth. His hands pressed her closer against him, brushing lightly along her spine until her whole body vibrated with a wild uprush of feeling that she could not control.

'I'm not playing games, Copper,' Sven murmured. 'I'm deadly serious.'

Deadly was the operative word! The pressure of his kiss changed, and deepened, lingering with sensuous invitation over the full, soft curves of Tay's mouth, which parted helplessly with an instinctive response that was beyond her power to prevent.

His tongue came out and flickered lightly across her parted lips, and with growing despair, Tay felt herself begin to slip inexorably over the edge of the precipice

into the dreaded void below, from which there could be
no escape and no return.

Panic-stricken, she grasped at the only available
lifeline left to her to save herself from disaster. With a
superhuman effort, she wrenched away from him, and
babbled wildly,

'I *know* you're serious. You don't have to tell me.
You're serious about trying to make me change my mind
about the merger!' She felt Sven go very still, but she
rushed on regardless, 'I heard Scott order you to do it.
Make her fall in love with you, he said.' She mimicked
the hated words, that burned indelibly on her mind.
'She'll be like putty in your hands then, he said.' Shrilly,
she flung his Chairman's words like weapons in Sven's
face.

They ended on a high, hysterical laugh that choked
into silence on a sob.

'Tay, don't! It wasn't like that for me.' Sven's hand
reached out to her and she struck it away, hitting out
wildly against the demoralising effect of his touch.

'*Sven, don't,*' she mocked. 'Don't *bother*!' she flung at
him passionately. 'You're wasting your time. Far from
making me change my mind, you've made me more
determined than ever that I'll have nothing to do with
you or your hateful firm!'

Now the dam had burst the words poured out of her in
an unstoppable spate, and she hurled them at Sven like
poison-tipped darts.

'I'll see Hilliard's go bankrupt before we merge with
Fieldings,' she panted. 'You can go back to Scott
Fielding and tell him so. Tell him you've failed in the job
he gave you to do. And you can tell him, too, that I hate
and detest you for the methods you've used to do it!'

And bursting into tears, she buried her face in her
hands. The edge of the precipice had given way, and she
hurtled helplessly towards whatever fate awaited her in
the dark depths below.

She loved Sven. She could no longer hide from the fact herself. Humiliatingly, she could no longer hide it from him. He had succeeded superlatively well in the task which Scott Fielding had set him to do.

The storm took a long time to pass.

Harsh sobs racked Tay's slender frame, and when at last they began to subside she felt drained and empty, purged of all feeling except for an agonising pain that lodged in the region of her heart and a burning anger against Sven that did nothing to alleviate the pain.

She was aware of a handful of soft lawn being pushed into her fingers, and she closed them round it automatically and mopped her streaming face. She did not attempt to give the handkerchief back to Sven, but kept it clenched in her trembling hands, holding on to it like an anchor.

'Tay?'

Her sobs faded into catchy, uneven breaths, and Sven turned and reached out both his arms to draw her into them. Underneath his healthy tan his face had a curious grey tinge, but Tay's swimming eyes were too blurred to notice.

'Don't touch me. Don't even *speak* to me!' Frantically, she pushed his hands away. 'If you do, I'll get out of the car, and walk all the way back to Mombasa!'

She turned her head away from him and closed her eyes, shutting out the sight of Sven's face, lest by looking at it she might weaken and melt into those waiting, open arms, where she longed to be.

Every nerve-end of her screamed out to beg him to tell her that she was mistaken, that his lovemaking had nothing to do with the dubious politics of business deals and mergers. That he had meant every word. Every kiss.

Her eyes longed to fly open, to search his face for what she hungered to see there, and it took every ounce of her willpower to keep her lids clamped tightly together, while her body remained rigid against her seat.

She must not weaken now.

No matter how Sven might protest his sincerity, she would know that he was lying. And if she pretended to believe him, to luxuriate in his lovemaking that her whole being ached for with a hunger that would never be assuaged, she would only invite more heartbreak and more pain.

After what seemed a lifetime of waiting, Tay sensed him draw away from her, and the movement made her heart feel as if it were being wrenched in two.

The leather upholstery of his seat crunched as he straightened, and her safety-belt slid round her.

She held her breath, but Sven did not attempt to touch her. The two locks made faint clicks as he drove the belt-ends home, and then the car engine started into life, bringing back the cool breeze through the windows like a balm against her tear-scalded cheeks, as the car rolled on through the idyllic scenery that she would remember with anguish for the rest of her days.

Tay recalled little of the rest of the journey into Malindi, except for the smooth, soothing motion of the vehicle, and an unutterable weariness that made her feel as old as history, like a dried-up shell that would never be capable of feeling joy in anything again.

She roused and sat upright in her seat when the car braked to a halt for the second time, and saw they were parked in front of an hotel.

'We're booked in here for the night,' Sven said briefly, and Tay returned in a taut voice,

'In single rooms, I hope.'

She saw Sven's face tighten, but she did not care. At the moment, she felt beyond caring about anything.

'In single rooms,' he agreed, and added, as if the words cost him an effort, 'Linkman's meeting us here in three-quarters of an hour. You needn't come if you don't feel up to it.'

But she answered grimly, 'I'll be there. If you're going

to do a deal with this man, I aim to see that you don't short-change Hilliard Engineering in the process.'

Which left Sven in no doubt as to her opinion of his tactics, nor what she considered him to be capable of.

He slanted her a steely look as he rounded the car, granite-faced, and reached in to help her alight.

'Stay away from me! I'll manage for myself.'

With a vicious jab of her fingers, Tay unlocked her seat-belt, and without waiting for it to react, she thrust it savagely away from her, venting her feelings on the hapless strap because nothing—but nothing—was bad enough to vent what she felt about Sven.

'Tay, wait,' he began as she scrambled free from the car. 'I can explain.'

Tay turned on him, her eyes blazing.

'Wait for *you*?' she sneered. 'I've got better things to do. Like keeping a business appointment. And as for your explanations, you can keep them. I don't want to hear them. I wouldn't believe them if I did,' she flashed.

And ducking under his arm that held the door open for her, she ran into the hotel before the threatened tears could start again and proclaim just how completely he had succeeded in what he had set out to do.

Copious splashings of cold water, and a careful application of make-up, effectively disguised most of the ravages. Shadows still lingered in her eyes and darkened the pallor of her cheeks below them, but to a casual observer they might not be obvious.

She marched downstairs to the small conference room allotted for their use with her head held high.

Samual Linkman proved to be a middle-aged, stout, and an extremely shrewd bargainer. After a perfunctory greeting, he handed Sven and Tay typed sheets of questions to act as an agenda, and said decisively, 'I'll go over the details of the engine with you, Miss Hilliard. Then, when we've finished, you can jot down any details you think I might have overlooked, while I discuss the

possibility of modifications to the camper furnishings
with Mr Diamond.'

It was a strictly business atmosphere, sterile of any
emotion, and Tay grasped at it eagerly to salvage her
shattered senses.

During the next hour and a half their client went over
every inch of the engine with her in minute detail, and
Tay answered his questions mechanically. She was so
well versed in each aspect of the engine, from its
inception on the drawing-board right through to its
actual production, that she was able to quote facts and
figures with a confident authority that left her questioner
quite obviously impressed.

By the time he reached the end of the typed list Tay
thought ruefully that Samuel Linkman could not have
overlooked a single nut or bolt.

He then proceeded to go through another, equally
long, list with Sven. While the two talked together, Tay
conscientiously penned in some notes on one or two
points that she considered might benefit from being
enlarged, but the comprehensive nature of their discussion had left few points uncovered, and with the notes
soon finished, there was nothing else left for her to do.
Except to watch Sven.

She loved him.

It was almost easier, now she had admitted the fact to
herself, she discovered with a feeling of dull surprise.

She had had the usual incursions into the realms of
romance, but until she met Sven she had succeeded in
remaining heart-whole. Now, she had lost her most
precious possession—her heart—to the one man in the
whole of her acquaintance who was least worthy of it.

And who did not want it for himself.

Would she ever regain possession of it? Tay wondered
wearily.

Lunchtime came and went, and still the two men
talked on. Tay let it go. In her present state of mind she

felt as if the very sight of food would be enough to make her sick. Even the coffee, brought in by a helpful waitress to sustain them, remained cooling and untouched at her elbow.

The hands of the clock crept towards four by the time their client declared himself satisfied.

'Now we must eat,' he announced, and insisted upon Tay and Sven joining him for tea. Over the meal, he shed his business role, and became human.

'You're not eating, Miss Hilliard,' he noticed. 'Would you like something else? Something different?' He made as if to beckon a waiter, and Tay raised her hand in an urgent disclaimer.

'No, really, I'm not hungry. It's the heat,' she stammered the first excuse that came into her head. 'We've been rushing about during the last few days. The Trials . . .'

'You've been working too hard,' their host chided. 'Why not take an hour or two off while you're in Malindi, and relax? We've got the finest beaches in the world here.' With an expansive wave of his hand, he invited them to share his boast. 'Take a swim and cool off, or sit in the shade of the palms.'

If only things had been different between herself and Sven, what bliss it would be to accept his invitation! If only things had been different.

'I've got a letter to write, first,' Tay prevaricated, before Sven could back up their host's suggestion, and she escaped to the writing-room the moment the meal was over.

It was occupied by several industrious scribblers already, who plied their task in a silence reminiscent of a library, and Tay joined them with a sigh of relief.

Sven could not press his explanations on her in here. She would be safe until dinner-time. Gratefully, she sat down at one of the small writing-tables, pulled a sheet of notepaper towards her, and began, 'Dear Jean . . .'

Her friend would be surprised to receive a letter from her, but it had to come to an end at some time. Reluctantly, Tay stuck down the flap of the envelope and stamped it, then dropped it into the posting-box in the lobby.

Twice during the course of the last couple of hours she had been aware of the door of the writing-room opening and Sven's head peering through the gap. Each time, she resolutely kept her eyes on the page, and continued steadfastly to write, and each time, after a few minutes, the door closed and he went away again.

But she could not put off meeting him again for ever.

Dinner would be as good a time as any. No matter how miserable she felt, she could not continue to starve, and a crowded restaurant would inhibit Sven's activities.

Scott joined them at dinner, primed by success to continue his battle with Tay.

'I've had an excellent day,' he remarked to Sven as he sat down. 'What about you?'

He could only be describing the business deals. Tay had not heard him comment in such glowing terms on the wonderful sights in the game reserve the day before.

'Very good,' Sven reported. 'We've got Linkman safely hooked.'

The same did not apply to herself, Tay thought, and listened in tight-lipped silence as Sven went on,

'Linkman's ordered twenty campers for the start of the tourist season next year. There's every likelihood of more orders coming along. When the other tour operators see the kind of luxury vehicle he's running, they'll want the same in order to compete.'

'The more the merrier,' nodded Scott, and turned hard eyes on Tay. 'This should be enough to convince you of the necessity to merge with us quickly,' he pressed her, and his look was as cold as the glass of iced grapefruit juice she held in her hand. 'You'll never be able to expand in time to cope otherwise,' he said with arrogant confidence.

Tay braced herself to resist the pressure that she had known would come. 'You already know my answer on that score.'

'You're impossibly stubborn!' Scott snapped. 'I always did say it was a mistake to allow women into business.'

'Why? Because they might have more courage than the men, and challenge your feudal rule?' Tay flashed.

'Your sex are incapable of making a sensible decision,' Scott declared. 'You allow your hearts to rule your heads. You let sentiment get in the way of business.'

'You'll never be guilty of that.'

It was one thing nobody would ever be able to accuse Scott Fielding of doing. He was hard all the way through. In his own way, he was as inhuman as Andrew Gleeson.

'At least I've got a heart,' Tay said, and knew an agonising pain that it was no longer true. Sven owned her heart. All that she had left for herself ws an empty, aching shell.

'If you won't merge willingly, I'll force you to sell out,' Scott threatened. 'I'll make you regret it.'

The gloves were off now, and he turned on Tay like a Goliath, certain that he had her at his mercy, and ruthlessly prepared to crush any remaining resistance from the tiny valiant who refused to admit that she was beaten.

'Your father's received countless orders for his engines alone, as well as those we'll need for our campers,' Scott bulldozed on. 'You'll have to expand hugely to be able to cope, and you haven't got the money to do that without my backing. If you continue to resist me, I'll drive you into a corner, so that you'll be glad to sell out to me at any price.'

'That's enough, Scott.' Sven's voice cut sternly into the diatribe, and his voice was harsher than Tay had yet heard it. 'Leave her alone,' he ordered the other man abruptly.

His Chairman looked at him in astonishment.

'Leave her alone?' he echoed. 'Are you out of your mind, Diamond? I haven't even started on her yet!'

'You've finished, so far as Tay's concerned,' Sven disabused him.

'You've both finished, so far as I'm concerned.' Tay rounded on them both, her eyes glowing with an anger that set them alight.

'Sven lied to you,' she informed him. 'He hasn't had a good day. He hooked Samuel Linkman, but I'm the fish that got away. Oh, he tried his best.'

She threw Sven a withering look, and wondered fleetingly if the pallor of his face was caused by the peculiar effect of the fluorescent lighting. But the last of her concerns now was for Sven. She addressed herself to him in molten tones.

'Tell Scott you've failed with me,' she cried. 'Tell him I saw the hook underneath the bait, and refused to swallow it. Tell him . . .'

'Stop it, Tay!' Sven cut sharply across the flood. 'Sit down, and eat your dinner.' He turned gimlet eyes on Scott. 'For once, let's all try to behave in a civilised manner, and forget business during the meal.'

'Civilised?' sneered Tay. 'You don't know the meaning of the word. All either of you think of is business. Making money. And you don't care what methods you use to get it. The animals in the game reserve behave in a more civilised fashion than you do. And as for eating my dinner here, I hope I never have to touch another mouthful of food in your company. It makes it taste bad,' she declared. 'I'll have my dinner in my room.'

And pushing back her chair, she hurried out of the restaurant before either of the men could get up from their seats.

The meal, when it was delivered to her room, served

only to intensify the leaden weight that rested inside her. Tay had no tears left with which to ease it. She felt as if she had shed her lifetime's supply on the journey to Malindi that afternoon.

After a while, the maid came in and removed the tray, and Tay locked the door behind her when she left. It was a purely symbolic gesture, since no subsequent knock sounded on the panels demanding entry.

Perhaps when Sven said, 'Leave her alone,' he meant it literally. Perhaps putting her in purdah was another tactic to force her to change her mind.

Slowly, Tay began to undress.

She unclipped the brooch from the shoulder of her dress to put it in her small travelling jewel-case, and discovered her hands were still trembling. Her fingers fumbled, and the smooth setting of the brooch slipped through them, ejecting it on to the floor. She stooped wearily to pick it up.

The opaque stone of the tasteful costume jewellery stared back at her, and Tay looked at it indifferently. It did not matter if the fall had damaged it. Whenever she travelled, she never took with her anything of value. Her precious jewellery, the family heirlooms which had belonged to her mother and now belonged to Tay, was all safely in the bank at home.

Her mother's jewellery . . .

For a moment Tay's mind refused to register the enormity of the thought that flashed through it. Her father was adamant that it should not be touched. But it was the only way left open to her. With the money she could raise on the jewellery her father could finance any expansion that was necessary to keep the firm afloat, while remaining independent of Scott Fielding and his Board.

The stones of the heirlooms were genuine. The settings were antique. And from the amount of money for which they were insured, Tay knew that at auction the pieces would fetch a fabulous sum.

She would have to do it secretly, without her father finding out. And quickly, the moment they returned home. She would get in touch with Christie's.

Tay flinched from what her parent would have to say when he discovered what she had done, but by then it would be too late. Once the jewellery was sold, the pieces would be irretrievably lost, and faced with a *fait accompli* her father could plough the money into the firm.

Tay's revitalised mind clicked into action, planning exactly what she would do. She snapped the lid of her jewel-case shut on the costume pieces that, from now on, would be her only adornment. In the heirlooms lay the only solution to Hilliards' dilemma.

And also the key that unlocked an unsuspected reservoir of tears, which soaked her pillow before, exhausted, she finally found merciful oblivion in sleep.

CHAPTER TEN

THE car that took them to Mombasa the next morning was chauffeur-driven.

'I'll sit in the front with you,' Tay said to the man, and allowed him to help her into the passenger seat, ignoring the rear door held open for her by Sven.

The presence of the chauffeur would restrain Scott and Sven from any attempt to pressure her on the journey, she realised thankfully.

Not that it mattered now. They would no longer need Scott Fielding's money, and anything he or Sven tried to do would be so much wasted effort on their part. She felt tempted to tell them so, to fling her secret in their faces for the sheer satisfaction of watching her bombshell burst, but with an effort she denied herself the pleasure.

It was essential to keep her father in ignorance of what she intended to do, because he would do everything in his power to stop her. Tay hugged her secret to her, and took her seat in the car, strengthened by her decision into showing an outward calm of which she felt quietly proud.

True to her word, she had breakfasted in her room that morning, and only descended to the car at the very last minute, in order to avoid her unwelcome travelling companions for as long as possible.

They had not been many minutes on the journey before the atmosphere between Sven and Scott Fielding percolated through to Tay. Even with her back turned towards them she could sense the almost unbearable tension from the back seat, that pointed to a major row between the two men.

Had Sven incurred his Chairman's wrath because of what he had said at dinner last night? Scott Fielding was

not a man to accept opposition lightly, and Sven's
unexpected championship of Tay must have come as a
considerable shock to the older man.

But if Sven lost his place on the Fielding Board as a
result it would not mean bankruptcy for him. Sven would
not be obliged to sell his most precious possessions in
order to survive.

Conversation in the car was almost non-existent
during the journey, and the silent battle being waged
behind her between two implacable wills made an almost
audible clash, so that in spite of the beauty of the scenery
and the presence of the chauffeur that should have
allowed her to relax and enjoy it, Tay was thankful when
they reached Mombasa.

Morgan Hilliard was waiting for them in the lobby of
his hotel, and his face was wreathed in smiles. He looked
almost carefree, Tay thought wonderingly. He must have
received substantial orders for his engines to make him
look like that.

She hoped he would look even happier when she had
obtained the means for him to produce those engines
without recourse to Scott Fielding's assistance.

Tay responded warmly to her father's kiss, making up
for Scott's dry, perfunctory handshake and Sven's short,
'Have you heard from Jorgssen yet, Morgan?' which
accompanied his firm grip, as if he could not wait for the
greetings to be over to find out what he wanted to know.

Jorgssen?

There was the name again. The name of the film
producer, Tay remembered belatedly, and wondered
what Sven's godfather could want with her father.

'I had a cable this morning,' Morgan Hilliard was
telling Sven in a delighted voice. He turned to Tay. 'I've
got some wonderful news to tell you, love. Come in here,
where we can talk privately.'

He ushered her into a small side-room, where coffee

was already laid out for them, and Scott and Sven
followed closely on her heels.

'What news?' Tay eyed her father curiously as she
accepted her cup.

'The very best,' Morgan Hilliard assured her. 'Sven
Jorgssen wants to hire our entire museum of miniature
cars for several months, for a film he's making. And
guess what?' His eyes glowed excitely. 'He's prepared to
pay us a hundred thousand pounds for the privilege!'

'A hundred thousand?' Tay stared at her father with
widened eyes. 'I don't believe it.'

'Neither did I, at first. But it's all here, in the cable.'
Her father laughed excitedly. 'Just think, Tay. We've got
enough funding to expand twice over, and then some.
Imagine it. There'll be no need for us to merge with
anyone.'

There would be no need, either, for Tay to sell her
mother's jewellery, she realised with a dizzy sense of
relief.

'This is your doing, Diamond!' Scott Fielding shouted.

He slammed his coffee-cup down on the table with a
crash that made them all jump, and sprang to his feet.
His face was livid. 'You're behind this,' he accused Sven.

'Right in one,' Sven acknowledged, and Tay stared at
him, bewildered by the unexpected turn of events.

What double game was Sven playing now?

'I'll see your head roll for this,' Scott grated. 'I'll call an
emergency meeting and have you thrown off the Board!'

'Haven't you forgotten something, Scott?' Sven asked
him suavely. 'My head's no longer yours to guillotine. In
case it escaped your notice, I told you last night that I
didn't intend to renew my contract with you. Which
incidentally expired last night. So I'm no longer a
member of your Board as from then.'

'You were a member when you started up this film
business,' Scott blustered. 'I could sue you, Diamond, for
working against the Company's interests.'

'No chance,' Sven retorted. 'This deal was a family matter. It's nothing whatever to do with Fieldings. My godfather had already borrowed my own vintage Hilliard for the same film, and he wrote to ask me if there were any drawings available from which he could make mock-ups of other vintage models for his shots.'

'So that's why you were so interested in our museum when I took you round our works that day?' exclaimed Tay, remembering.

'That's why,' Sven nodded. 'When I wired my godfather about it, he couldn't believe his luck when I told him you not only had actual models, but working ones as well.'

'It seems a crazy price to pay, just to hire them.' Tay frowned suspiciously, unwilling to trust anything in which Sven had a part.

'He would have to pay an even crazier price to have mock-ups made,' Sven returned. 'When my godfather's making a film, his budget has to be seen to be believed. The price he's paying will be worth every penny to him.'

'I'll make you pay an even higher price,' Scott Fielding threatened.

His face had taken on a mottled, purplish tinge which, even disliking him as she did, began to alarm Tay faintly.

'Come, gentlemen.' Her father held up his hand authoritatively. 'This is no time for unseemly quarrelling. Rather, I should say, it's time for mutual congratulations.'

'I don't see ...' Scott blustered.

'Then you should,' Morgan Hilliard retorted. 'We've had an absolutely marvellous success at the Trials, thanks to Sven and Tay. We've both netted very large orders for our firms as a result. And by not having to fund our expansion, you've also saved yourself a heavy outlay of capital, and you'll still get our engines from us as a valued customer.'

Adroitly, he used the only argument—money—that

was likely to strike a chord with Scott Fielding.

'Make sure you give our orders priority, and deliver them on time, or else,' snarled Scott, in no way appeased at seeing his quarry escape his clutches.

'We'll do that, never fear,' Morgan Hilliard returned. 'With the firm orders I've already received from other companies, I can expand our work force as well as our premises. I've got enough work here in my briefcase,' he patted it lovingly, 'I've got enough work to keep us going at full stretch on engines alone for at least the next three years, which will help us carry the car business side until it begins to pick up and make a profit for itself again.'

Which told Scott that he was by no means Hilliard's only customer, and they would not be reliant on his orders alone to keep them afloat.

'Sit down, and have a fresh cup of coffee, and let's talk business, there's a good fellow,' Morgan Hilliard went on, magnanimous in victory. 'I've still got only a sketchy idea of how many campers you've sold so far. We need to work out between us what engines you'll want, and when.'

Scott Fielding hesitated for only a second, but the lure of business won, as always, and he sat and reached for his own briefcase.

'I think we're *de trop* here for the moment,' Sven said, as the two spread their papers on the table between them.

'That's right, you two go along,' Morgan Hilliard bade them. 'Scott and I will take until lunchtime to sort out the details of our production runs.'

'Can't I help you?' pleaded Tay. The last thing she wanted was to be flung into Sven's company again.

'Not really. I can do it just as well for both of us,' her father refused her offer. 'Sven can't join in,' he pointed out, 'because he's no longer involved. It's a good opportunity for you both to have a few hours off together. I'll bring you up to date on what's been decided during the flight home,' he promised.

There was no help for it but to leave the two Chairmen together.

Reluctantly, Tay walked ahead of Sven back to the hotel lobby. The bookstall caught her eye, and she hurried over to it. She would choose a paperback, she decided, and spend the morning stretched out on a lounger in the hotel garden.

'If you want some mags to read on the plane, why don't you buy them at the airport?' Sven enquired. 'They'll have a better choice there.'

'I'm going to read in the garden until lunchtime.' Tay threw him a look that would have daunted a lesser man.

'What a waste!' Sven exclaimed. 'There's all this marvellous scenery going begging, and you want to bury your head in a book. I know a superb beach, just a short run from here.'

'I don't feel like running,' Tay quelled him, adding silently, only away from you. Out loud she finished, 'Anyway, I thought Malindi had the best beaches,' as if that settled the matter.

'Let's go and find out if we agree with Samuel Linkman,' Sven invited. 'Come on, Copper,' he urged. 'You can't spend the morning sulking amid scenery like this.'

'*Me*, sulking?' Tay flashed, and Sven grinned.

'That's more like it,' he approved. 'But there's no point in fighting me either, now. I'm neutral, remember?' he reminded her. 'I'm not involved any more.'

How easy it was for Sven to opt out of things. How easy for him to shrug, and say he was not involved, and walk away, leaving the wreckage he had created behind him, for someone else—herself—to try to repair as best she might.

Her heart would be involved, and the scars it bore would still smart, for as long as it continued to beat.

It thudded uncontrollably now as Sven cupped his

hand round her elbow and coaxed, 'The car's waiting outside.'

Why did he have to touch her again?

Despairingly, Tay felt her muscles turn to water, felt the familiar, quick leaping of her senses that started at Sven's fingertips, and ran like a forest fire unchecked through her veins, scorching, burning. Bringing her alive, and destroying her at the same time.

Destroying her will to resist him.

'The car's waiting,' he prompted.

If the car was waiting, so would the chauffeur be, she remembered, and the flood of relief helped to steady her and to bring the fire in her veins at least partly under control, so that she was able to respond with commendable steadiness,

'In that case . . .'

It was humiliating to discover how eager her heart was to spend these last few sun-drenched hours with Sven. Tay's mind scorned her for her weakness. But as if of their own accord, her feet followed the path her heart wanted to tread, and walked her beside Sven out to the waiting car.

They sat decorously apart on the back seat, and once he had helped her inside the car, Sven made no attempt to touch her again. It was a relief and an emptiness at the same time, and an indication, if she needed one, that now Sven no longer had an axe to grind with his lovemaking he no longer had any desire to make love to her.

It was the final humiliation, and extinguished the fires in Tay's veins to a smouldering glow that only anger and resentment kept alive.

The chauffeur dropped them at another hotel, and Sven gave the man some money to buy himself a coffee and a snack while he waited for them, and enquired if Tay would like one as well.

When she shook her head he said, 'Let's go down to the beach,' and she assented willingly enough. If the beach belonged to the hotel, there would be other people there, too.

Sven led her along twisting paths that he seemed to know well, through terraced gardens, down to a stretch of dazzling white sand. with palm trees throwing grateful shade. The Indian Ocean made a sparkling blue ribbon bordering the beach, laced some distance out by a line of white breakers marking a coral reef.

Impulsively, Tay stopped and slipped off her sandals, and swung them in her hand, crunching her bare toes luxuriously in the hot dry sand.

Sven took her other hand in his, and she jumped nervously. Now she came to look round her, she realised uneasily that the beach was deserted. Even the loungers placed in the shade of the palm-trees were unoccupied.

She paused with her back to a trunk, reluctant to go any further alone with Sven, although it was not Sven she feared now, but herself.

'It's a lovely view,' she remarked tritely, using it as an excuse to stop walking.

To her dismay, instead of looking at the view, Sven turned and placed a hand on each side of her against the trunk of the palm-tree, effectively fencing her in, and he looked down long and searchingly into her face.

Tay stared up at him, startled, and her courage oozed as he stared back for a long time without speaking.

'Hadn't we better go back?' she stammered. 'We mustn't walk too far. We haven't got all that much time to spare. I—I think I might like a coffee, after all.'

Her voice trailed away, and her eyes were wide and wary, fixed on Sven's face.

'What are you frightened of, Copper?' he asked, and his eyes bored into her face.

Instead of answering him, Tay looked frantically from side to side, seeking some means of escape.

She glanced surreptitiously at Sven's right arm, It was higher up the trunk than the other. If she moved quickly, she might be able to duck under it, and run before he realised what she was about to do.

Agilely, she ducked. With winged feet, she fled across the beach towards the hotel.

'Tay!' She heard Sven call, but she did not turn round. She ran on, making for the coffee-lounge where there were other people.

She fled as the fleeing impala had done from the menace of its pursuer, running for its life, as she ran now for her own, because if Sven held her again, kissed her again, her heart would surely die within her.

It hammered wildly against her ribs, bringing an excruciating stitch that made every panting breath an agony. The soft sand slipped under her bare feet, dragging at their soles so that each step was an effort, slowing her down.

She should have known she had no hope of outdistancing Sven. His long legs brought him up behind her, catching up with her easily, and his arms reached out to capture her, turning her to face him.

Tay stared up into his face with wild eyes.

'Let me go!' she panted. But instead of letting her go, he held her all the more closely and demanded to know again, in a voice that said he would not be gainsaid,

'What are you frightened of, Copper?'

She could have said, 'You.'

She could, with equal truth, have said, 'Myself.'

The lean, hard line of his frame pressed against her. She could feel his taut muscles through the thin cotton of his tropical whites. And she could feel, too, the wild beating of her own heart that fluttered erratically against the strong, steady beat of his, choking her throat so that she found it impossible to answer him; impossible to think of an answer, with her mind in a whirl.

'We've got a lot to talk about,' Sven said, when she continued to remain silent. 'There's a lot of explaining to do.'

'I don't want to hear your explanations.' Tay grasped at the remaining shreds of her courage with both hands. 'I don't want to listen. I want to go back to the hotel—back to the car.'

She struggled to free herself, looking round her wildly for some sign of hotel guests. If only someone would come, Sven would have to loose her then, let her go. But from the lack of human life, the hotel might as well not have been there. Except for herself and Sven, the pale sands were as empty of life as a desert island.

'You're not going anywhere until you've heard me out.' Sven's jaw jutted at a determined angle that told Tay there was to be no escape.

'I won't listen. You can say what you like, but I shan't believe you!' she shrilled. 'Save your explanations for Olive!' She hit low because she had no other weapon with which she could defend herself.

At the mention of Olive's name, Sven's eyes narrowed to angry slits.

'If I set eyes on that woman again,' he growled, 'I might be tempted to do what Lance should have done years ago, if he'd only been man enough.'

'And what might that be?' sneered Tay.

'Give Olive the spanking of a lifetime, until she learns to behave herself.'

'Why, because she led you on, and then wouldn't deliver?'

'Olive? Lead me on?' Sven gave a short bark of a laugh that all of a sudden turned to one of genuine amusement. 'I'd have to be naïve not to see through Olive Poulton,' he said scornfully. 'In a way, I suppose I ought to admire her,' he added surprisingly. 'Initially, she did it for Lance.'

'For Lance? The plot thickens. Tell me more,' Tay invited sarcastically.

'Lance got the wife he deserved,' Sven obliged her. 'He only married Olive for her money. Which is why he doesn't bother too much about her affairs, so long as she doesn't provoke an open scandal that might damage his career. There's no love lost between them. Lance used Olive's money to buy himself a place on the Fielding Board because he hasn't got the personal drive to achieve such a position for himself, and he's prepared to overlook a good deal so long as he's got access to her bank account.' There was a mixture of scorn and pity in his voice as he finished, 'Poor fool! He imagines that money can buy him everything.'

Sven's eyes lingered on Tay's fresh face with a look in them that set her heart doing crazy acrobatics in her breast. To steady it she said hastily. 'What about Olive?'

'She's got the better business brain of the two. If only she'd been allowed to join the Fielding Board as well as Lance, it would have kept her out of mischief, and I've no doubt she'd have made a more useful contribution to the firm than Lance. As it is, because of Scott's antediluvian ideas about women in business, she was obliged to work in the background to bolster Lance.

'By having an affair with you?' Tay snorted.

'Initially, by trying to make it look as if she'd got an affair going with me,' Sven corrected her. 'Scott's a strange mixture,' he mused. 'He's willing to go to the most unspeakable lengths in the sacred name of business, but he's oddly scrupulous when it comes to marriage. Olive somehow got the idea in her head that if she could make it look as if I was leading her on, it would discredit me in Scott's eyes, and give Lance a better chance of becoming his second-in-command.'

He smiled grimly.

'When she discovered I wouldn't play her game, it seemed to drive her mad. She can't understand any man not being fascinated by her womanly wiles,' he said, and there was utter distaste in his tone and his look. 'It was all to no avail, really,' he added, and again pity added to the mixture. 'So far as I'm concerned, Lance is more than welcome to become Scott's deputy.'

'Sour grapes,' Tay taunted.

'Not so,' Sven denied. 'I refused to renew my contract with Fieldings, so I put myself out of the running for the job, not the other way round.'

'What made you do it?' Curiosity got the better of her.

'I don't like Scott's methods of doing business,' Sven answered, and surprisingly Tay did not doubt his sincerity on that score, but before she could comment he went on,

'I don't mind a fair fight. That's what business is all about. But I don't like Scott's underhand methods, and the other two—the other three, if you include Olive—are just as bad as he is. They all deserve one another,' he finished with feeling.

'You might as well include me among them,' Tay said. 'You think I leaked that photograph to the Press. And then you accused me of putting sugar into the camper petrol tank.'

The injustice of it still rankled, like a sore that refused to heal.

'I thought at first you might have leaked the photograph,' Sven admitted slowly. 'You'd got your back to the wall, fighting for Hilliard's very existence, and you were desperate. But even then,' he admitted slowly, 'I couldn't believe you would be capable of doing such a thing. Olive is. She's completely amoral.'

'For once, we're in agreement,' Tay bit out. 'If Olive . . .'

'As a matter of fact, Olive didn't do it,' Sven said quietly. 'Andrew Gleeson did.'

'Andrew Gleeson?' Tay could not hide her astonishment. '*That* cold fish?' she exclaimed.

'Cold, calculating, and quite determined to succeed Scott in the chair at Fieldings,' nodded Sven.

'By why leak his own firm's photograph? What good

did he think that would do him?'

The plot was becoming more tangled by the minute. Tay felt as if she were listening to some bizarre drama with no script, an insoluble plot and who knew what ending?

'Because Gleeson guessed you'd get the blame,' Sven explained. 'You dropped the photographs, if you remember, and when you picked them up, you had the opportunity to secrete one in your handbag if you wanted to. Gleeson used the opportunity to try to put a spoke in the wheel of the merger.'

'But he wanted the merger—he said so himself, at the meeting. He tried to put pressure on Dad and me.'

'He paid lip-service to the idea of the merger, to please Scott. Lance was no threat to him. He isn't capable of running a complex organisation the size of Fieldings, and when I insisted on a yearly contract only, Gleeson gambled on the probability that I wouldn't be a permanent rival to his ambitions.'

'Surely in that case, he'd got no one else left to fear?'

'It left your father, if the merger went ahead,' Sven said surprisingly. 'Morgan's a brilliant man.'

'You don't have to tell me that,' Tay said proudly, and Sven nodded grave agreement, and continued,

'It wouldn't have taken Scott very long to see the advantages of appointing your father to the Fielding Board if the merger had taken place, which would have destroyed any hope Gleeson entertained of becoming deputy Chairman.'

'How did you find out about the photograph?' Tay wanted to know, still hardly able to absorb what Sven was telling her.

'I shook it out of that rat-faced little reporter,' Sven grinned at the memory. 'After he talked, it wasn't too difficult to get a confession out of Gleeson as well.'

'Did you tell Scott?'

Exit Andrew Gleeson if he had. Olive would not need

to fight for her husband any longer. There would be no
one left but Lance to take the post.

Sven shook his head. 'No, Scott's wily enough to be
able to protect his own interests. Gleeson's an able man
in his own sphere. There'd be nothing gained by queering
his pitch. If he seconds Scott, he'll be loyal enough to
Fieldings, because it won't be in his own interests to be
anything else. There's nothing now to prevent him from
achieving his ambition.'

'Which leaves the sugar in the petrol tank,' Tay
reminded him tightly.

Sven had accused her of that as well, and she could not
forgive him for his suspicions.

'Olive was responsible for that.' Sven sprang another
surprise. 'The security guard at the showrooms smelled
perfume when he went in to investigate the opened door.
The next time Olive walked by his office he recognised
the smell and came to me with his story.'

Sven had not seemed to be too surprised when he
learned from the mechanic what ailed the small camper,
Tay remembered. He had been angry, very angry, but not
surprised. The incongruity of his reaction had not struck
her until now.

'I suspected something of the kind might happen,'
Sven explained his puzzling reaction. 'That was why I
changed the position of the campers in the showrooms.
At a glance, it isn't easy to tell the two vehicles apart, and
if Olive was vindictive enough to try sabotage, I had to
make sure she didn't harm the big camper, which we
wanted for the Trials.

'Why should she want to sabotage either of them?' Tay
protested. It seemed as incomprehensible to her as
Andrew Gleeson leaking the photograph to the press.

'Out of spite, because I wouldn't play her odious
game,' Sven shrugged, and added contemptuously, 'she'd
make a terrible burglar. She not only wears a perfume
that needs a hurricane to remove the reek from your

nostrils, but she spilled sugar all over the showroom carpet while she was pouring it into the petrol filler. It was a dead giveaway that something was amiss, and justified my suspicions.'

So that was why Sven had toed the showroom carpet, the day they set off on the Trials. Tay had thought at the time he was kicking the carpet out of pure temper, because she insisted upon going along with him in Ken Wallace's place.

Some of the pieces of the jigsaw were beginning to form a scrappy sort of picture, but the wide gaps still left served only to increase her frustration.

'What are you thinking about, Copper?' Sven wanted to know as she remained silent, brooding over what the gaps might reveal.

Tay tilted back her head and looked up at him, frowning.

'I think ... I think ... I don't know *what* to think!' she exploded on a rush of pent-up breath.

The bits of the puzzle which had been fitted in did nothing to solve her own personal problem, and she took refuge from it in attacking Sven.

'I smelled Olive's perfume at the poolside,' she reminded him, 'but you didn't believe me when I told you she pushed me into the pool. Yet you believed the security guard.'

'Like you, I didn't know what to think,' Sven answered. 'It was difficult to believe that even Olive would go to such lengths, But I decided to keep an unobtrusive eye on you, just in case.'

He had not been all that unobtrusive, Tay remembered, but she let it pass, and Sven went on,

'Afterwards, I heard you arguing with Olive in the lodge on the game reserve. And then when I came up behind you on the veranda above the water-hole, I saw the look in your eyes. Just for that moment, you were afraid. You thought it was Olive, and you knew exactly what she was capable of. Women sense these things in another woman.'

'And instead, it was you,' said Tay in a flat-sounding voice.

'It's a good job it was me. Instead of just watching out for you, the fright on your face goaded me into taking positive action. As soon as we got back to the hotel, I cornered Olive and Lance together, and we had a blazing row about the whole affair. After which,' he said with satisfaction, 'the only decent thing left for Lance to do was to take Olive back home by the first available flight. And after my interview with Gleeson shortly afterwards, he was glad to follow them.'

'And then there were two. Scott, and you,' Tay counted in a barely audible voice.

'Not Scott and me. *You* and me, Copper,' Sven contradicted her, and his voice softened, and became indescribably gentle. '*You* and me,' he repeated, rolling the words round his tongue as if he found the sound of them good to listen to.

His arms tightened round Tay, straining her to him. His dark head bent above her, blotting out the sea, and the sand, and the white-lace combers that marked the coral reef.

'*You* and me, Copper,' he repeated hoarsely, and took her lips by storm.

For a second Tay lay in his arms, stunned, too shaken by the onslaught of his kiss to resist him. It was bliss. It was torture. It was an agony too great to be endured.

Realisation returned, and with it panic.

'No, Sven. *No!*'

A strangled cry broke from her lips, and she began to struggle in the circle of his arms, striving like a trapped bird to break free.

'You don't have to make love to me now,' she cried. Her face was as white as the combers. 'You don't need to kiss me any more. It isn't necessary, now.'

'It's as necessary to me as breathing,' Sven muttered thickly, and his lips ravaged her cheeks, her hair, her eyes, anywhere they could reach, as Tay twisted her face frantically from side to side, to try to escape their demands.

'Can't you understand?' she cried. 'The merger's off. It isn't going to happen.' She hammered at his broad chest with her tiny beating fists, trying to break through his incredible non-comprehension. 'You don't have to make love to me any more, to make me change my mind about the merger.'

'I wasn't trying to make you change your mind about the merger,' Sven raised his head, and stared down into her face as if it were Tay who did not comprehend. 'I changed my own mind about that during the Trials. Why do you imagine I wired Jorgssen about the model cars if it wasn't to give your father a chance to make some quick money and escape Scott's clutches? Jorgssen doesn't actually need the cars for another six months or so.'

'Then why . . .?' Tay began perplexedly.

Sven shrugged. 'I could have put up the money myself, but you were so suspicious of me, I knew you'd fight against accepting it, because you'd suspect the motives behind it.'

'You promised Scott you'd make me change my mind about the merger. Don't try to deny it,' Tay cried as Sven made as if to speak. 'I heard you tell him so myself.'

Would she ever forgive Sven for making such a cold-blooded promise? Would the sun ever stand still?

'When I promised Scott I'd make you change your mind, he thought I meant about the merger. I didn't. I meant, about me.'

'About you?' Tay frowned. 'Why should you want to change my mind about you?'

'Because you disliked me. You mistrusted me on sight. And you'd got the lowest possible opinion of my motives.'

'Things haven't changed then, have they?' Tay countered. 'So why?'

Sven answered her simply. 'Because I loved you. So I *had* to make you change your mind about me.'

The sun must have gone to her head. Or else he was taunting her, being deliberately cruel and twisting the knife in her heart that was already bleeding to death from a wound that could never be staunched.

'I fell in love with you at the Federation Dinner,' Sven confessed. 'You looked like a queen in your green and silver gown. I hated Michael Burk for monopolising you.'

It *was* true. She *was* hearing him say . . . Incredibly, unbelievably, Sven loved her. He *had* meant every word, every kiss.

Tay stared up at him with eyes from which the shadows were fast disappearing, and incredulous hope that still did not quite dare to believe struggled to take their place.

Sven's eyes glowed with the fire of his love, but his face was as white beneath its tan as her own, indicative of his suffering because he had not managed to win her love.

'Tay, darling!' His kisses were a desperate entreaty on her mouth, begging it to speak the words that he thought it would never utter, 'Will you let me try to change your mind about me?' he pleaded. 'Will you give me a chance?'

He crushed her to him, and hid his anguish in the soft, warm pillow of her curls.

'Tay—my darling Copper! I love you, I love you,' he whispered brokenly.

A shudder that defeated even Sven's iron self-control racked his tall frame, and a strangled groan burst from his mouth as he buried his lips in her fiery curls.

Tay could bear his agony no longer.

'Don't, Sven. Don't,' she begged, and reached up tender hands to clasp round his head, holding it against her upturned face.

Her lips clung to his, seeking to heal the agony and silence the groan. Their mouths locked and held, Tay felt the smouldering fires burn into hot flames inside her, and willingly she let them burn.

Her heart reached out to embrace the flames as her arms embraced Sven. Her lips burned against his mouth wih a fiery intensity, communicating all the hope and the yearning that had been bottled up inside her.

It exploded now in a star-burst of passion that rocked them both with all the agony and ecstacy of a love that had been for too long unexpressed. For a long moment of suspended time they clung together, and then Sven roused, and Tay felt the tension grow like a brooding storm inside him.

'Tay?' His eyes searched her face hungrily, in spite of her kisses, still unsure. They were over-bright, and they clung to her clear gaze as if to a lifeline. 'Can it really be true?' he asked her hoarsely. 'You wouldn't . . .' he swallowed, 'you wouldn't be doing this for a joke, just to torment me?'

She had suffered too much torment herself to have any desire to inflict similar misery on the man she loved.

'I wouldn't torment you,' she whispered. 'I love you too much.'

Sven's face radiated joy. 'What fools we've been,' he exclaimed, 'to waste so much time.'

He wasted no more. With eager arms he crushed her to him. With seeking lips that were uncharacteristically hesitant at first, and then blissfully confident as Tay eagerly gave back the response they yearned for, Sven plundered their sweetness greedily, as one who tasted nectar for the very first time.

'Will you marry me, Tay?' he begged her humbly. 'I won't know a moment's peace until you're truly mine. If you should change your mind . . .' A spasm passed across his face at the unbearable possibility. 'I can't go on without you. It's you or no one for me,' he muttered.

'I'll never change my mind.'

With glowing cheeks and shining eyes, Tay rested back in his arms and gazed up into his face, her eyes lingering lovingly on each dear, familiar feature, that stern, harsh face whose lines gentled into a wonderful softness, because he was looking at her.

Tay's face lighted with a roguish look, and she smiled suddenly.

'You're stuck with me for life,' she warned him, and loved the laughter that made his blue eyes dance.

'For life, and after. For ever,' he vowed, and sealed his promise in the most convincing way he knew.

The white combers rolled in the distance, larger now as the tide began to turn. It crept slowly across the pale sands, as if reaching out to share the happiness it saw there, as a long time later Sven teased,

'You came along as my navigator on the Trials. You've got the job for ever, now.'

'You didn't want me to go along with you on the Trials,' Tay could not help reminding him mischievously. 'You tried to stop me.'

The hurt was behind her now, and it no longer mattered.

'I didn't want you to come, because I didn't trust myself,' Sven confessed.

'I didn't trust you either.' Tay chuckled at the memory.

'I know. That's why I had to go carefully,' he said. 'It took all my strength not to rush in and carry you off. You were like a wild, shy creature. I knew if I was to have any hope at all of winning you, I had to be patient. I knew that if I made any impulsive move, it might frighten you away for good. And I daren't let that happen.' He crushed her in his arms. 'I couldn't contemplate life without you,' he said tensely, and the tremor found its way back through him again. 'If you only knew what it cost!' he groaned, 'the night I held you in my arms, when the hyenas raided the camp on our first overnight stop . . .'

He broke off abruptly, overwhelmed even now by the strain of what that night had cost him.

'I'm glad I saw the game reserve with you,' Tay sighed contentedly.

'We'll come back for our honeymoon,' Sven promised with an indulgent smile.

'Oh, Sven, could we? I can't wait.'

'Neither can I,' he murmured, with a significant undertone that brought a rosy flush to her cheeks that made his eyes kindle. 'In fact, I won't wait any longer than it takes to have the banns read,' he declared masterfully. 'That'll just give me time to help your father get his expansion going, before I finally join the Diamond Line. And then,' he punctuated his promise with kisses, 'we'll have a whole month's honeymoon, just you and me alone, away from the world in the game reserves. We'll make it our own special paradise.'

But the glow in his eyes, as he bent his head to claim Tay's lips again in a long, lingering caress, said he already held his own personal paradise within the circle of his arms.

Bewitched in her dreams she awoke to discover the face of reality

The same dark hair, the same mocking eyes.
The Regency rake in the portrait, the seducer of Jenna's dreams had a living double.

But James Allingham was no dream, he was a direct descendant of the black sheep of the Deveril family.

They would fight for the possession of the ancestral home. They would fight against desire to be together.

Unravel the mysteries in
STRONGER THAN YEARNING,
a new longer romance from
Penny Jordan.

AVAILABLE FROM FEBRUARY 1987. PRICE £2.95.   W❶RLDWIDE

ROMANCE

Variety is the spice of romance

Each month, Mills & Boon publish new romances. New stories about people falling in love. A world of variety in romance — from the best writers in the romantic world. Choose from these titles in February.

ROSE-COLOURED LOVE Amanda Carpenter
GATHERING OF EAGLES Angela Carson
STREET SONG Ann Charlton
RECIPE FOR LOVE Kay Clifford
THE UNPREDICTABLE MAN Emma Darcy
THE MARRIED LOVERS Flora Kidd
A ROGUE AND A PIRATE Carole Mortimer
THE LOVE ARTIST Valerie Parv
SUNSET AT IZILWANE Yvonne Whittal
BRIDE OF DIAZ Patricia Wilson
***STAIRWAY TO DESTINY** Miriam MacGregor
***SLEEPING TIGER** Joanna Mansell

On sale where you buy paperbacks. If you require further information or have any difficulty obtaining them, write to: Mills & Boon Reader Service, PO Box 236, Thornton Road, Croydon, Surrey CR9 3RU, England.

*These two titles are available *only* from Mills & Boon Reader Service.

Mills & Boon
the rose of romance

ACCEPT 4
MILLS & BOON
ROMANCES
ABSOLUTELY FREE

...after all, what better way to continue your enjoyment of the finest stories from the world's foremost romantic authors? This is a very special introductory offer designed for regular readers. Once you've read your four **free** books you can take out a subscription (although there's no obligation at all). Subscribers enjoy many special benefits and all these are described overleaf. ▶▶▶

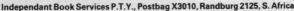